SHIFTERS OF BLACK FOREST RIDGE: QUINN

SEDONA VENEZ

WANT FREE SEDONA VENEZ BOOKS?

Sign up for Sedona Venez's Newsletter and receive FREE BOOKS. In addition to the free stories, you will also get special pricing, exclusive previews and news of new releases.

GET A FREE SEDONA VENEZ BOOK!

Join Sedona's mailing list to be the first to know of new releases, free books, special prices and other author giveaways.

https://sedonavenez.com/free-book

CHAPTER 1
QUINN

When I stepped inside the empty Cauldron Saloon, Freya was standing behind her bar, putting away drinking glasses.

"So?" she called out. "How did the video conference call with the Shifter Council go?"

"It was a shit show," I replied, sitting down at the bar. "They're blaming me for Clancy. And they resent the fact that his actions have become their problem to clean up." I sighed heavily. "Clancy has now been added to the Council's most-wanted list."

Before the Clancy incident, my position as alpha of the Ridge town and my Bane pack was highly respected by the Shifter Council—a secretive group of alpha leaders from various shifter breeds that governs the shifter world across the globe. But now they questioned my ability to run this town and pack effectively, all due to the Clancy clusterfuck.

Freya threw her arms up in the air. "There was no way you could have known he would do what he did."

Guilt slithered through me for failing him. Clancy was no stranger to me. My childhood friend and former military like me, Clancy had it all until he caught the feral sickness and then disappeared into the Ridge's rain forest. Now there was nothing I could do to save him.

"Maybe if I'd kept a closer watch on him, I would have known when he slipped out of town. Preventing him from killing those humans."

Just thinking about the video footage the Council had sent me made my blood run cold. The sheer brutality Clancy exhibited while attacking and killing the two human males sent a chill down my spine. His only saving grace was not harming the human female.

Freya poured two shots of BF Home Brew before sliding a glass to me. "Quinn, Clancy is feral, and that's not your fault. Now he has to pay the price for killing those humans."

"But wasn't it my fault?" I clipped out before downing the contents of my shot glass in one swallow, reveling in the burn as it went down. "I'm the alpha of this town. And if I can't protect my pack, friends, and townsfolk, then what good am I as their leader?"

Now my failure could bring down not only me but my family, pack, and town as well.

"You're being too hard on yourself," Freya said. "You're not to blame for the feral sickness. Unmated male shifters have been going feral for eons." She sipped her own BF Home Brew before continuing, "Everyone, including the idiot members of the Shifter Council, knows that the only solution to the feral problem is to find unmated males their fated mate."

"That's easier said than done."

The feral situation was not new to this town or to the shifter world. It was a fact that all unmated males would eventually get the feral sickness—and go feral; it was just a matter of time if they lived without their fated mate. But no one understood why unmated female shifters did not suffer the same fate. Not that there were a lot of female shifters in the first place.

She pointed at me. "Exactly. That's my point. The Shifter Council should be focusing on finding a remedy to the feral sickness problem, especially given the fact that they, too, are unmated. Without a mate…"

"They will turn feral. So will I and all the members of my pack." My inner beast growled at my words. "Someday the Council's Trackers will have to kill me and my pack." My words held no bitterness even though I'd spent years trying to find my fated mate without success.

"The remedy is fated mates," Freya said, refilling my glass. "We find them, then we stop unmated males from going feral. Even feral shifters like Clancy can be cured of their sickness if they find their fated mate."

"Freya, if I don't get the feral problem in the Ridge under control, the Council said they would." I gulped the shot. "And we both know how the Shifter Council handles feral shifters."

Her expression was one of disdain. "By sending their top Trackers to hunt and kill them."

As with most things, the Council dealt with the feral issue with an iron fist. They terminated all feral shifters. There were no second chances. I knew that when the Trackers found Clancy, they would kill him.

I locked eyes with Freya. She was my mother's best friend, a powerful witch, and one of the few who I respected in the Ridge.

"Freya, I'm here because I need your help." I swallowed hard. "If you cast that spell you told me about—"

She cut me off. "No. We talked about this. There is no way in hell I'm casting that spell."

It said a lot that a powerful witch like Freya, who was the leader of the town's coven, had serious reservations about casting such a spell. But that didn't stop me from pushing the issue.

"This is our only solution," I gritted out. "Unless I find the mates for all the unmated males in this town, and fast, the Ridge is fucked."

"You can't be serious." She laughed dryly. "You want me to trust the solution given to me by a strange spirit who waltzed into my bedroom in the middle of the night?"

"Yes," I barked. "She told you it was the remedy to our

unmated males problem." I curled my hands into fists with frustration. "That when you cast the spell she gave you, it will call the fated mates of all unmated males to the Ridge."

Freya's stoic expression turned grim. "Quinn, I can't trust a spirit who refused to tell me her name or why she picked me to give the mating spell to. All the spirit would tell me was the purpose of the spell and that it was ripped out of a book of spells." She blew out a breath. "When I asked her who wrote it, she didn't answer or tell me why the spell had been removed from the book in the first place."

I finally threw my arms up in the air in my exasperation. "Can't you figure out a way to validate the origins of the spell?"

She shook her head, annoyance etched on every line of her face. "The spell is ancient text. And without seeing the spell book the page was torn from, I can't validate anything. But what I do know from analyzing the words is that this spell is pretty powerful."

She paused, eyeing me. "Quinn, if I cast this mating spell, I don't know what else I could be calling. Honestly, what the spell is supposed to do and what it will do could be completely different. I'd be messing with the universe with no clue about the ramifications. Are you really willing to accept the consequences as the alpha of this town?"

My irritation swelled. "I have no choice. Desperate situations call for desperate measures."

I'd already failed Clancy. I couldn't risk failing another unmated male in my pack and town.

Disapproval turned down the corners of her mouth. "And what if the spell doesn't work?"

I narrowed my eyes, and my nostrils flared. "Then we tried, which is better than doing nothing."

Freya's lips pressed into a thin line. "If I cast this spell, and it works, the results will not be instantaneous. It will take time, as magic does."

"I understand," I clipped out.

She stared at me, worry shining in her eyes.

"Freya, you know I wouldn't ask this of you unless I had to. You and I know this is the only way forward."

She sighed heavily. "So be it. I'll call the members of my coven."

CHAPTER 2
IMANI

ONE YEAR, SEVEN MONTHS LATER...

Sheer determination—along with too much caffeine—were all that kept my ass going.

"Come on, baby, make Mama proud. Just hang on to the road," I begged my old compact car that had carried me through so much already.

My car's wheels skidded alarmingly on the snow-covered serpentine road that had twists and turns and dipped and arched over the imposing waves of the crashing sea that flanked both sides of the freeway.

I squinted through the drifting snow as it slapped against my windshield, faster and harder than the wipers could push it away. The wind battered my car as I navigated the icy, winding road, constantly squinting through snow and darkness.

Black Forest Ridge, Alaska, was somewhere ahead on this road and with it, hopefully, my next place to live and work until the season changed. Then I'd leave in search of somewhere new.

But the longer I drove through the inky darkness, the more I wondered if I'd made a terrible mistake in making this long, nerve-racking journey. I couldn't figure out why I'd been second-guessing every decision I made lately. Maybe it was the emotional exhaustion that had settled into my bones since I turned forty two weeks ago. Or maybe it was the fatigue that tore at me after having barely slept since leaving New York a few days ago, with a trunkful of my last remaining belongings and a wad of cash stashed in my messenger-style leather handbag. But what I was sure of was that my only hope of a safe landing at—fingers crossed—my temporary home was the online job posting for an executive chef position at a bed-and-breakfast in a place called Black Forest Ridge, Alaska.

But what if I don't get the job?

I shook my head. *No, Imani. That's not an option.*

Gripping the steering wheel, I tried to calm the anxiousness tightening in the pit of my stomach.

Dammit. I need this job and the money.

I was also freaking out because Black Forest Ridge, Alaska, wasn't on any maps. Nor did it show up on my phone's GPS. According to the internet, physical maps, and the local roadway authority, the town simply didn't exist.

How is that even possible?

Piper Bane, the B and B owner, had given me vague directions over the phone. Those had put me on this thruway.

"Don't forget. Black Forest Ridge is situated approximately thirty minutes from the city of Anchorage. Just follow my directions, keep driving on the thruway, until you see the tunnel in the mountain. It leads to the Ridge," Piper had specifically informed me. "You can't miss it."

My knuckles ached from gripping the steering wheel and fighting the gusts of wind. I'd expected a short drive but had gotten hours in the pitch-black darkness and a wicked snowstorm.

Continuing to drive, I relaxed slightly when I spotted the passageway and drove through it, happy to at least find a reprieve from the storm. I slowed inside the dark tunnel, the beams of my headlights the only thing guiding me.

In Piper's directions, she'd mentioned the tunnel, so I took it as a good sign that I was heading in the right direction.

When I made it out of the tunnel, my body slackened with relief just a second before crisscrossing lines made of white lights shimmered in front of my car.

What the hell?

I pushed my foot down on the brake pedal firmly, but my vehicle sped up instead of stopping, barreling me right through the Vegas-like light show. Loud popping sounds echoed around me, and a weird pulse of energy tingled against my skin.

The bright white lights vanished.

My cell screen flickered out.

Seconds later, so did my headlights.

"Shit! Shit. Shit," I hissed while applying the brakes quickly, trying to stop, but my car continued moving forward at a fast clip.

Something big and black dashed in front of my car. I jerked the wheel hard, screaming as my car hydroplaned off the road and into a tree.

My body slammed against the seat belt, and the aging pulleys gave way before my head slammed against the steering wheel with a thump.

CHAPTER 3
IMANI

Groaning, I woke up, trying to get my bearings. I sat back gingerly, wiping my hand across the fogged-up driver's side window. "Dammit." My car was off the road, with rain sluicing over the vehicle.

Rain? What the hell happened to the snow?

No. How long have I been here?

Quickly, I did a personal inventory.

My head hurt where I'd smacked it, and my neck ached from being jolted forward. I could feel the seat belt bruises throbbing on my shoulder, hip, and across my breasts. Cautiously, I checked my collarbone. I hadn't broken anything. Next, I felt around for my cell, finally finding it lying against the passenger seat. The screen flickered on when I swiped it. "Okay. That's something."

Grabbing my messenger bag, I checked inside, sighing with relief when I saw my money was still there. But when I tried to turn on my car, nothing happened—no power.

"Time to get the hell out of here," I muttered. With my bag in one hand, I unbuckled my seat belt. Slinging the bag across my body, I opened the driver's-side door, shoving it wide and clambering out.

As I stood on the road, icy rain pelted down on me, chilling through me as I realized the front end of my car was smashed against a tree.

"Damn. I'm lucky I survived."

When I checked my phone, hoping to call a tow service, I didn't have a single bar. *Just my damn luck.*

There was nothing else I could do but start walking in the same direction I had previously been driving, hoping the road would lead into town. My boots weren't ideal for hoofing it, but it didn't make sense to start digging through my luggage in the dead of night on an isolated stretch of road for something more practical to wear. Sighing, I started trekking away from my car in search of life.

My pace quickened as the frigid rain beat against my body. It didn't take long for my thick, curly hair to come undone from the bun, and the leather of my peep-toe ankle boots chafed.

Just tough it out, Imani. Keep moving.

My feet were aching and growing numb at the toes and ankles as I slogged along. Mud caked my toes, and pebbles kept working their way into the boots and bruising the bottoms of my feet. I wanted to sit down and bawl my eyes out, *but nope, just keep your ass moving.*

I continued walking until I came across a fork in the road. I remembered from Piper's directions that she'd told me to go left at the fork. So that's what I did on foot.

A deep growl pierced the air. I froze, peering around in alarm, but I couldn't see far enough up or down the road, and an impenetrable wall of blackness stretched between the trees that stood on both sides of the road.

With trembling fingers, I turned on the flashlight function on my phone, desperately shining the light around.

Don't freak out. Keep it together.

The faint light showed me nothing ahead or to either side that moved. But something was stalking me. I could feel it.

Shivering with trepidation, I turned around, aiming my light straight ahead. A chill ran down my spine when I saw the massive bulk crouched in the middle of the road.

What the hell?

Is that an animal?

The enormous beast rose and was now standing on two legs like a human.

But that was not human.

It had clumped, thick fur—the color between black and white —covering its entire body.

It looked like… Bigfoot.

I blinked and blinked again.

Imani, chill out. There's no such thing as Bigfoot.

I swallowed hard over the lump in my throat as the thing emitted an angry-sounding growl.

Oh hell no…

Turning on my heel, I ran, then stumbled and ran again. I raced down the road as mud and small stones slid under my feet. The rain intensified. Behind me, I heard the booming roar of the animal.

My muscles, already battered from the crash, protested as I sped through the icy night. But my legs couldn't move fast enough. I knew that my desperate sprint would eventually flag from exhaustion, but I had to give this shit my all because from the rhythmic thumping and thrashing noise behind me, I knew the Bigfoot thing chasing me was huge and was probably a lot faster than me.

The best that I could do was hope that I got to safety before it caught up to me. I ran flat out despite the pain of the exertion.

The animal growled again, this time louder, and then I recognized the sound from one of the many animal wildlife shows that I was addicted to watching. It was a damn wolf.

How could that monstrous thing be a wolf?

Maybe it was a mutant—a mix of a wolf and Bigfoot.

Shit. If that thing caught me, it would maul me to death and eat my remains. No one would even notice I was missing. I had no family and no friends. But I'd be damned if I'd let that animal eat me. Nope. I had too fucking much I still wanted to do with my life.

Jolts of adrenaline raced through me, pushing me forward even harder. With one arm swinging by my side and the other clutching my cell, I fought the temptation to duck into the trees. Maybe that would have worked to lose a human, but a mutant Bigfoot wolf had to be better at moving over rough terrain than I was.

I ran, ignoring the bruises my feet were getting from flying stones, the cold, and the rain. A feral roar came up fast behind me. I didn't know what I'd done to piss off the mutant, but it seemed determined to destroy me.

The trees thinned as I ran alongside them, and the forest soon opened out again into a valley with a long driveway bordered by streams and shadowy forest. I stuck to the path of the driveway until it curved past the edge of ranchland, leaving me running beside a white stock fence.

Glad as hell that I had always made a point of keeping fit, I grabbed the top of the fence and swung myself over with all my strength, barely sticking the landing on the other side. I didn't know if the fence would deter the mutant or not, but I felt a little better putting it between us.

A huge ranch house stood perhaps a quarter mile up a hill that rose from the roadside, growing steeper as it ascended, forming part of the valley slopes.

Praying I would make it in time, I scrambled up the muddy incline, half-blind from darkness and rain, my cell phone light providing little warning of the obstacles ahead.

Yes. The ranch house lights are on.

But is anyone home? And will they answer the door?

I heard the mutant's labored breathing behind me, then the sound of splintering wood as it crashed into the fence.

Come on, please, just one lucky break on this shitty night.

The beast growled before I heard a grunt and more cracking of wood.

Oh, sweet baby Jesus. Don't eat me, mutant Bigfoot.

Fear sent me stumbling up the hill even faster. I was almost within reach of the ranch house's sprawling front porch and, beyond it, the door.

Can I get there in time?

Wood cracked again as if boards were snapping, and then I heard the harsh rasp of the beast's breathing and the heavy thud of its feet on the muddy grass coming up behind me.

Fuck. My. Life.

CHAPTER 4
IMANI

Desperately, I threw myself up the porch stairs, tripping, righting myself, slamming against the door. I pounded on it frantically.

"Help!" I swallowed hard. "Let me in. Mutant Bigfoot wolf is going to eat me!"

Heavy footsteps approached the door, and I heard locks and bolts being opened on the other side. A moment later, someone yanked the door open. I stumbled forward before a pair of hands gripped my forearms and righted me.

With lungs burning, I tilted my head back to look into the man's eyes.

He wasn't handsome, but he had a face that was hard to look away from. With short black hair, he possessed rough, masculine features. Inky black brows slashed over piercing, sky-blue eyes.

He continued to stare down at me as though he were memorizing every line and contour of my face.

I opened my mouth to speak, but the only thing that came out was a high-pitched squeak.

He sniffed. His eyes narrowed.

Oh God. He thinks I stink.

Embarrassed, I pulled away from him and launched myself onto the closest thing inside—a brown saddle-leather couch.

Inside, the space was so warm it made my chilled skin sting. I panned my eyes around the bright area. The far side of this room had a full, large kitchen. On the north side was a larger dining room area, where a long table, overhung by an antler chandelier, seated a group of men the size of linebackers, who were now staring at me as if they'd discovered a new species and didn't know if I was dangerous.

A heavy silence descended on the room, and the only thing missing was the loud chirp of crickets.

My heart battered against the wall of my chest. *Shit.* And they're massive, like they could lift a damn truck.

They were all scowling, and each strong-featured man wore a long-sleeved button-up work shirt, jeans, and cowboy boots, tanned as if they spent lots of time outdoors rounding up cattle.

I swallowed hard. Sweat coated my clammy hands and prickled under my arms. *Oh God. Did I jump out of the frying pan into the fire?*

My breath quickened, going into panic mode.

Are they a cult of crazy cowboys?

I'd watched enough horror movies to know that a lone female surrounded by big, strange, angry men never had a happy ending. And given their heavily muscled bodies, they could subdue me easily—well, not that easily because I'd give them one hell of a fight and crush some nuts while I was at it. They could kill me and bury me in the backyard or violate me in several unmentionable ways, and then…

Someone cleared his throat loudly. It was the guy who had opened the door for me. His lips were in a line—neither a smile nor a scowl. Our eyes locked, and my exhaustion and fear faded into the background.

Shit, he's big, scary, and oddly sexy.

He seemed bigger than the others around the table. He was a wall of muscle in a dark blue button-up work shirt rolled to his elbows, heavily broken-in jeans, and cowboy boots. His entire body was one sheet of pure, rippling muscle, and he had to be at least six seven.

There was an oddly uncharacteristic butterfly feeling in the pit of my stomach as I considered him from head to toe and back again, which took me a while. He wasn't my type, but I couldn't take my eyes off him. An image of me on all fours with him fucking me from behind flashed through my head and made my pussy pulse with need.

Where the hell did that come from?

Mr. Big's nose twitched. He tilted his head to the side as if he were examining a scientific experiment gone horribly wrong. My stomach plummeted. Or maybe he was trying to figure out how many black garbage bags he'd need when he and his cult of cowboys got ready to kill me by chopping up my body.

Shit! Way to go, Imani.

Why couldn't I just be happy with my abysmal life in New York?

If I'd never left, I sure as hell wouldn't have gotten chased down by Bigfoot wolf or be minutes away from being killed in some random man's house by a cult of cowboys.

I inhaled a slow, deep breath and struggled not to make it obvious that I hovered on the brink of hyperventilating.

"Calm down, female," Mr. Big demanded. "You're safe."

I pointed at Mr. Big. "Don't call me female. My name is Imani. And please close the door. There's a mutant Bigfoot wolf out there the size of an elephant!"

"Mutant Bigfoot wolf?" Mr. Big asked.

I snapped, "Yes! And I didn't drive all the way from New York to get mauled to death by the beastly monster, so please close the door."

He slammed the door and then locked it. Turning, he stared at me. And like an idiot, I just gawked at him.

A tall woman wearing all black attire, with worry in her eyes, hurried into the room, making a beeline for me. She had the same features as Mr. Big and the same black hair, except peppered with gray. "Jesus. You're soaked through," the woman commented. "Poor thing." She clucked her tongue. "Come over near the fire to warm up." She pointed at the massive stone fireplace in the middle of the room that effectively divided the room into a larger formal living room.

"Thank you," I croaked before standing up and limping in that direction. When I reached the fireplace, I gasped, feeling relief and pain. My fingers and toes felt like they were burning from the sudden return of warmth.

My gaze flicked over Mr. Big, then to the men still sitting around the table.

"Will you stop gawking?" Mr. Big ordered the men with a deep, rumbling voice that would have been a lot scarier in a less calm tone.

"But she's a—" one of the men replied.

Mr. Big cut him off. "Tonight's meeting is canceled due to unforeseen"—he flicked his eyes to me—"matters." Then he looked back to the group of men.

The men muttered to one another and then got up as one. None of them bothered to grab coats as they ambled past the older woman before heading out the door.

"And while you're out there," Mr. Big shouted after them, "don't forget to check around for signs of… Bigfoot."

My eyes narrowed when I heard a snicker from someone in the group, followed by a sarcastic-sounding, "Yeah, Bigfoot," response from one of them.

Do they think I'm making this Bigfoot thing up?

Boots thumped against the wooden floor as Mr. Big strode over to where I stood shivering. "You all right?" he asked.

I looked up at him, taking in his big blue eyes. I blinked after a moment, realizing I was eye-fucking him—again.

His shoulders completely dwarfed me, but he needed them that size to support his long, thick neck. And oddly, his physical proximity affected me in strange, sexual ways.

Heavily muscled, his biceps looked like boulders. He could

have palmed the entire back of my head with one huge, thick-fingered hand, and as I lifted my face toward him, I wondered what it would feel like if he kissed me. A moan escaped my lips.

What the hell is wrong with me? I'd been celibate for years, yet here I was, acting like I wanted to climb Mr. Big like my own personal tree.

Mr. Big inched forward slightly, inhaling loudly.

I frowned. *What's with the sniffing?*

He cleared his throat loudly before asking, "What happened?" He gestured to me.

I snapped back to the matter at hand—me, looking a hot mess while dripping mud and rainwater all over the ranch house's beautiful wooden floor. I frowned at my jeans, now dipped in mud from the knees down. My blouse was plastered against my full breasts, leaving nothing to the imagination. My favorite leather boots were caked with dirt.

"Shit. I'm so sorry for the mess," I babbled.

His eyes studied me. "I'm more concerned about that goose-egg lump on your forehead."

I touched my forehead and winced as pain radiated through my head. "I'll be okay," I said nonchalantly, even though the room was spinning slightly, making me feel nauseated.

He scowled. Apparently, he didn't appreciate me down-playing my injury.

"I was in a car accident," I blurted out. "And then there was this giant Bigfoot wolf chasing me—"

"There's no such thing as a Bigfoot wolf," the man inter-rupted me.

"Really?" I snapped. "Well, then please explain what just chased me through your pasture?" I curled my hands into tight fists at my thighs.

His mouth tightened.

"You can't, can you?" I argued. "Look, I know what happened to me. I was being hunted by a mutant animal, because that wolf thing was unusually big, and it had red eyes." I shuddered just remembering the beast.

"You're not from around here." He tilted his head slightly. "How did you get here?"

I licked my dry lips. His gaze narrowed, locking on to my movement.

"I was following directions I got over the phone," I admitted. "I have an appointment with someone for an executive chef job up here, and I was just trying to reach town. But then there was this weird flash of lights that I drove through…" I swallowed hard just thinking about the craziness of that incident. "It was as if it sucked me and my car into some strange vortex, and then it spat me out the other side."

His eyes widened.

"Okay, yes, I know I sound crazy, but it's true." I swallowed hard because even I didn't understand what had happened to me back on the road. "Anyway, after that, the power to my phone, car, and headlights cut out." I frowned. "My car felt like it hit something. I jerked the car and drove into a tree."

The older woman shook her head, clicking her tongue. "Oh, poor thing. Let me go get you a towel to dry off. And something for that lump on your forehead." She looked at the big man. "Quinn, close your mouth. You're going to catch flies. Show our guest some hospitality instead." She strode over to a rustic staircase, which had a cast bronze twig-and-branch handrail that curved majestically up both sides of the front entryway before swaying up the stairs and across a second-story walkway that crossed the big, open space over the living room, and then she disappeared.

Quinn let out a grunt and stepped past me, grabbing a chair and dragging it near the fireplace. "Sit down," he ordered. "You look cold and tired."

Glancing down at my mud-soaked jeans, I grumbled, "I can't. I don't want to mess up your chair."

He let out an irritated growl, pushing the chair against the backs of my knees, forcing me to sit down. "Female, it's a chair. I can clean it."

I sat there blinking for a moment, both stunned and irritated. If I weren't so grateful to have a warm place to sit and be safe from the mutant wolf, I wouldn't have let the incident go without saying something. But I was exhausted, shivery, and in pain.

I rubbed my hands together to get warm, with teeth chattering and fingertips still burning a little. "It's July. Why is it still so damn cold outside?" I grumbled.

Ignoring my question, he demanded, "What in the hell is that on your feet?"

I peered up and saw Quinn standing over me again with a scowl on his face as he gazed down at my ruined footwear. It had taken me forever to save up for these designer boots, and now they were destroyed.

"Three paychecks of buttery Italian leather," I admitted.

Quinn huffed in annoyance before leaning down to grab my foot.

I stiffened. "What the hell are you doing?"

"Taking off these ridiculous things." He yanked off one boot before I could protest, startling me with his deftness.

His huge, callused hands enveloped my chilled foot, sending a tingling electric warmth racing up my leg. The foot massage left me lolling in my chair. My entire body swayed in time to the tender pressure of his fingers and palms on my foot as the pain and cold retreated. Frankly, it was weird that this giant of a man was rubbing my feet with all the attentiveness of a lover. But I didn't give a shit as long as he didn't stop.

Please don't stop.

My eyes slid closed, with everything in me focusing on the amazing sensation. They popped open when a low growl sound reached my ears.

"Was that you?" I squeaked.

He coughed. "Yes. Allergies." He gently dropped my foot

and grabbed the other, pulling off my other boot. This time, as Quinn rubbed the circulation back into my toes, I tried to distract myself by looking around.

The place was a little more rustic than I was used to, but everything about it spoke of expensive high quality. Heavy timber furniture, saddle-leather upholstery, thick log walls with contrasting soft, rich fabrics, and a variety of forged iron reliefs.

Fascinated, I stared at the artwork above the fireplace—it was a forged relief depicting three wolves, a jaguar, lion, tiger, and a bear, gathered around a raging fire like it was some sort of social event.

A moment later, I heard quick steps and then saw the older woman returning.

"Here you go, dear." She bundled a big, fluffy white towel around my shoulders. The woman lifted a well-manicured brow at Quinn, who abruptly stopped rubbing my feet and moved slightly away from me.

I grabbed the towel gratefully to rub it over my wet hair. "Thank you," I replied softly.

"It's no trouble," she chirped. "I'm worried about that bump on your head. We don't have any pain medication, but maybe a bag of cold peas pressed against it will fix it right up."

"It's okay," I answered. "I'm more concerned about warming up."

I liked the woman immediately because of the way she hovered with worry like a mother. The maternal care was foreign to me but welcomed. It was something I'd never experienced when I was young and growing up, bouncing from one foster home to another.

"You said you got directions?" the woman requested.

I cleared my throat. "Yes. I'm here for a job interview. I followed the directions as best I could, but unfortunately, I just didn't make it that far."

Quinn stared at me with a confused expression.

The woman's brows furrowed slightly. "That's strange." She

tilted her head, inspecting me. "What's your name, dear?" she asked. "And who gave you the directions?"

"My name is Imani Parker. I came here to be interviewed for an executive chef position at a bed-and-breakfast owned by a woman named Piper Bane."

Quinn and the woman exchanged startled looks before the woman offered a smile that looked a little forced. "Well, I'm Piper Bane. And I own a bed-and-breakfast that needs an executive chef. So maybe we can talk about that once you've recovered."

"Wait." I darted my eyes between the two of them. "You mean I actually made it to the right place?"

How the hell did I even do that?

"Yes, you did." Piper smiled and nodded. "Welcome to Black Forest Ridge, Imani."

CHAPTER 5
QUINN

Wait. What the hell?

Imani got directions to the Ridge from Mom?

Impossible.

I could tell from Mom's expression that she had never communicated with Imani.

I knew exactly what had brought her to my town.

I'd scented her the moment I opened my door.

Imani was my fated mate.

For shifters, the act of recognizing our fated mate was not science. We knew our mate by their distinctive scent and our unmistakable, primal attraction to the person.

Imani was the female I was destined to love, protect, and cherish for as long as I lived.

She was the one woman I'd searched for my entire life.

But instead of me finding her, she found me.

It had to be all thanks to the mating spell Freya had cast a year ago.

My cell beeped, and I tugged it from my front pocket. It was a text from my beta and the town sheriff, Rhett.

RHETT (TEXT): *We solved the mystery. Bigfoot is Sam. His scent was all over your shattered fence, but he's long gone.*

I bit back a growl. Not liking the fact that Samuel, a crazy son-of-a-bitch wolf-shifter with a habit of causing nothing but fuckery, was involved.

ME (TEXT): *Find him! He tried to hurt Imani.*

RHETT (TEXT): *Probably because he scented that she's a hybrid.*

The scent of her human and shifter blood was undeniable to any shifter. And if there was one thing most full-blood shifters like Sam hated, it was hybrids.

ME (TEXT): *Yup. And I won't put up with his shit. She's my fated mate.*

RHETT (TEXT): *WTF? Mate? But she's a hybrid…*

To most shifters—but not me—hybrids were viewed with disgust and hatred because they were considered weak, less-than abominations masquerading as shifters. But I didn't subscribe to that elitist nonsense. She was mine.

ME (TEXT): *I don't care. She's mine.*

RHETT (TEXT): *But how? Do you think it's Freya's spell?*

ME (TEXT): *My fated mate. A hybrid. Just waltzed into a town that's not on any map. What do you think?*

I didn't believe in coincidences, but she had been called here and not by my mother. However, I still needed Freya to officially confirm my suspicion.

RHETT (TEXT): *Well, congratulations. I'll tell the rest of the pack. But you know her presence means nothing but trouble. Especially once townsfolk get wind that a hybrid is in their town, the shit is going to hit the fan.*

ME (TEXT): *The Ridge is my town.*

RHETT (TEXT): *Bro, Tomato. Tomahto. Like I said… this is trouble.*

And it was trouble. Only my pack and Freya's coven knew about the mating spell.

ME (TEXT): *We'll deal with the townsfolk later. Now go find Sam.*

Imani's voice broke into my texting conversation, and I shoved my cell back into my front pocket.

"This is crazy," Imani commented, tucking her tight-corkscrew hair behind her ears. "I was driving forever and was lost. I don't understand how I got here." She frowned, moving her hand away from her hair.

"Yep, nothing but trouble," I muttered before stepping away from Imani and leaning against the wall beside my fireplace, balancing on my shoulder.

"Excuse me?" Imani replied, her eyes locked with mine without the demure lowering of lashes or sly flirtation I often experienced with other women.

Damn. Even her glare is a turn-on.

"Behave, Quinn," Mom demanded, glaring at me.

I huffed, annoyed. I wasn't used to pussyfooting around the truth. I wanted to tear the blinders off Imani's eyes. I needed her to know that she was now in a town filled with Others—a society of witches, vampires, shifters, and other supernatural beings—and that she was mine.

Mom smiled at Imani. "It seems my son has lost his manners."

Imani rebutted with "You can't lose something you never had." She checked her cell. "Damn! Still no signal." Her eyes narrowed on me. "Why is your cell working and mine is not?"

I shrugged even though the truth was that her cell wouldn't work because it wasn't on our private network.

She eyed me suspiciously before wobbling to her feet and giving Mom a slight smile. "Ms. Bane, I'd like to get out of Quinn's hair ASAP. Could you call me a car service to take me to the nearest hotel?"

"We don't have one," Mom answered.

"Excuse me?" She looked at Mom as if she'd just grown horns and a tail.

Mom shrugged. "We don't have a car service. In Black Forest, most people have a vehicle or just walk to where they need to go."

"Great." Imani frowned, her brows pinching toward the center.

"Imani—" I said.

Imani cut me off and directed her words to Mom. "Do you mind giving me a ride into town so that I can get a room for the night?"

Mom fidgeted from one foot to the next. "Um. Well…"

"She can't do that." I took a step toward Imani, struggling with every ounce of my being not to give in to the need and possessiveness warring within me. Primal instincts were trying to claw their way out. The struggle not to shift made my head pound.

Claim. Mate. Mine, my wolf growled.

Both man and beast wanted Imani like they'd wanted no other woman.

Shadows clouded Imani's eyes, making them appear darker. "Why not?"

"There's no hotel in town," I informed her. Well, technically, that wasn't true. We had a run-down motel called the Sleepy Skunk Motel that was owned and inhabited by the skunk-shifters, but I couldn't tell Imani that.

"You've got to be kidding me," she remarked.

"Nope," I returned, keeping my gaze on her beautiful face—rich, dark skin; full, bow-shaped lips; and a cloud of thick, corkscrew hair that puffed around her face. But it wasn't just her stunning looks that attracted me to her. The savage need that raced through me was more than physical—it was primal. Just being around Imani was like a full assault on my senses. Everything around me became more intense: sight, hearing, texture, and scents.

My inner wolf clawed at the edges of my mind, begging to come out and claim Imani.

Mine, my beast growled, but I ignored him.

She turned to stare at Mom. "What about your bed-and-breakfast?"

"It's still being renovated," Mom admitted.

Imani's shoulders drooped. "Where am I going to spend the

night?"

"Here," I blurted out. "I have an extra bedroom." I had to be losing my mind or was a glutton for punishment. *Why the hell didn't I just let Mom put her up for the night?*

"Nope," Imani answered firmly. "I'll sleep in my car."

"In your car that you crashed into a tree?" I snorted. The stubborn woman was beyond rational thinking. "That shit is not happening."

She stiffened. "And who's going to stop me?" she countered.

A tense silence stretched between us. She glared at me with a hard glint of steel in her eyes, as if she expected me to back down. Everything alpha and dominant within me rose to meet her challenge.

Her hard stare with the quirk of her eyebrow declared her authority and demanded my submission. *She has the wrong man for that shit. I'm alpha through and through, and I don't submit to anyone.* But I couldn't help imagining what it would be like to have a woman of such strength willingly submit to me. Giving herself to me for my keeping and pleasure.

My inner wolf growled with approval.

Lust raced through me at the vision of her curvy body pinned under me, her thighs spread wide as I pushed my hard and ready cock between her warm pussy lips.

Could she take me easily?

Or would her pussy only be able to take me inch by inch?

I stifled another growl, just envisioning her womanhood stretched around my cock as I buried myself inside her pussy.

Mom's voice broke my sexual fantasy. "Quinn will keep you protected, Imani."

Imani rolled her eyes. "No offense, Ms. Bane, but I can protect myself."

I like her, my inner wolf commented. *She's strong. Just what we need.*

Mom smiled. "Needing protection is not a sign of weakness, dear, especially when whatever chased you might still be outside. Frankly, you don't need to be traveling to my place this late at night, not with that big bump on your head."

Imani was quiet for a moment, as if in deep thought.

She finally spoke. "I guess I don't have many options before me." She paused and glared at me. "Thanks for the offer," she said in a saccharine tone that didn't fool me one bit. I'd pissed Imani off with my high-handedness.

"I take it you're not thrilled with staying with me," I stated, enjoying goading her.

"I'm positively giddy with joy." She bared her teeth in a grin that was wide and mean. "Can't you tell?"

Her feistiness amped up my arousal even as amusement quirked the corner of my mouth. "I'll show you to my guest bedroom."

"Imani, I'll see you bright and early in the morning," Mom called out as I escorted Imani across my living room.

"I look forward to it," Imani answered.

After crossing the room and walking up the stairs with her behind me, we arrived at my guest bedroom. I pushed open the door, turning on the light—for her benefit, not mine—before stepping into the large room.

"It's not much, but the sheets are clean and it's comfortable. It used to belong to my parents years ago. It could use some sprucing up."

"Quinn. It's fine." She looked down at her clothes with the layer of dried mud caked on them. "I have nothing to change into, and I'd hate to get this beautiful room dirty."

"I can get you something to put on for the night." I pointed to the far end of the room. "You have your own private bathroom. I'll be right back."

Imani swayed, legs giving way, and I caught her before she hit the floor. "Imani? Are you okay?"

"My head is killing me." She groaned. "I'm going to hurl."

Not wasting time, I picked her up.

"What are you doing?" she squeaked.

Ignoring her, I cradled her body against my chest as I stormed over to the bathroom.

"Put me down," she grumped.

I got her to the toilet just in the nick of time before she started vomiting. I held her steady with one hand, the other pulling back her thick hair, and she threw up again, then groaned and heaved. She finished throwing up and leaned against my body as if she didn't have the strength to hold herself up.

"God. This is so embarrassing," she remarked softly.

"There's nothing to feel ashamed about," I answered while holding her up, simultaneously closing the toilet lid so she could sit down.

"So says the man who had to hold my hair while I barfed." She steadied herself on the toilet. I stepped back, immediately missing the contact. "I can't believe I did that."

I didn't address her statement. I was more concerned about her being sick and me not having any type of human remedy to help ease her ailments.

"One second," I grumbled before grabbing a clean washcloth from the shelf, wetting it, and holding it out to her. "Here you go."

She took the cloth with a soft "Thank you." Slowly, she wiped her face before raising her gaze. "The injury to my head must be worse than I thought. I just got a little woozy, and the room spun." She frowned. "I hate to be more of a pain in the ass than I already am, but are you sure you don't have any pain relievers?"

"None. I'm sorry." As a wolf-shifter, I had no need for medicine. In the rare case that I was sick or injured, I would shift into my animal and then back to human form, and that did the trick for fixing what ailed me. And if that didn't work, I could call Izzy, who was a witch and a healer.

"Damn, this is going to be a rough night," she mumbled as she wobbled to her feet. "Whoa," she whispered, tipping forward.

Quickly I grabbed her, preventing her from face-planting onto the bathroom floor. "Let me get you to bed. You need to rest."

"No. I need to hop in the shower to clean off all this dirt and filth." Her mouth pinched. She had to be in a lot of pain.

I sighed. "I need your permission."

"Permission for what?" She stared up at me in confusion.

"To help you undress and then get you into the shower."

She gave me a suspicious look. "Uh. That's not happening."

I met her gaze. "I'll be damned if I let you slip and crack your head open on my bathroom floor."

"I'll be fine, Quinn." She grimaced. "If it makes you feel better, you can hover outside the bathroom, listening for signs of life."

I scowled. She wasn't in any shape to be left alone. I wanted to help her, but given how stubborn she was, that wouldn't get me anywhere.

"There're towels and washcloths on the shelf." I pointed to the corner. "New toiletries are in the vanity under the sink. Help yourself."

"Thanks," she whispered.

Reluctantly, I backed out of the bathroom, closing the door. I quickly strode out of the room, down the hall, and into my bedroom. I grabbed a T-shirt and sweatpants with a drawstring out of my dresser. Imani was tall and curvy, though nowhere near my size, but if she tied the string tight enough, my sweatpants would work.

Coming out of my room, I went back to the guest bedroom, placing the bundle of clothes on the bed. My acute shifter hearing picked up Imani's even breathing and the sound of the shower running. Sitting down on the bed, I waited for her to finish. It didn't take long before I heard the sounds of her getting out of the shower, then the sink running and her brushing her teeth.

My mind wandered to the vision of Imani naked, wet, with

her legs wrapped around my waist as I plowed my cock into her pussy.

Is she a screamer?

A dirty talker?

A scratcher? Or a biter?

I growled as my cock pulsed, and desire raced through my body. My wolf lifted his head with eagerness.

Imani's voice cut through my lust-induced haze. "Quinn?" she called through the door. "Is everything okay? I thought I heard an animal growl."

What the fuck is wrong with me?

"I, uh, left some clothes on the bed," I answered while rushing to my feet and fleeing the room before I did something that my human side would regret, but my beast would not.

Closing the door, I stood facing it, inhaling deeply, trying to get my lust under control. I felt like I was losing my mind. All my senses were on alert. Even in the hallway, my senses tingled from the memory of her deeply penetrating blend of vanilla and honey jasmine, caressed by sweet, sultry, musky undertones.

I felt dizzy with need.

My mouth watered with the desire to know the taste of her. If she were a full-blooded shifter, she would have known that I was her fated mate and would have begged me to make her mine. A request I would have gladly obliged.

But Imani clearly didn't know about our world or give a shit about the fact that if she refused to accept my mate claim, it was only a matter of time before I'd go feral.

CHAPTER 6
IMANI

I'd hoped that once I'd washed off the grime covering my body, I'd feel more like myself, especially now that I had a warm, secure place to sleep for the night. Instead, I felt unsettled and anxious.

I'd been through some crazy stuff tonight—between the accident and being chased by Bigfoot—which was the only reason I'd stayed here, rather than trudging back to my car to spend the night. But I had a nagging feeling that Piper and Quinn were more anxious about my being here than I was.

And what's the deal with Quinn?

First, he was rubbing my feet like my personal massage therapist, then he was acting like he couldn't wait to get rid of me, and now he seemed like he wanted to take care of me.

I'm getting whiplash from his hot then cold then hot behavior.

Worse, I couldn't understand why I gave a shit what Quinn felt about me. Yes, I found him attractive, but I damn sure wasn't looking to hook up. I was in Black Forest Ridge to work, not for sex.

While I finished drying off my body, the steam in the bathroom started dissipating. Lifting the towel, I wiped down the mirror. I took a quick look at my reflection. My dark skin glowed from the steam, but the knot on my forehead looked horrendous. But given my strange knack for healing quicker than most people, I knew from experience that, by morning, the knot would be half its current size. Carefully running the comb through my big, thick cloud of hair, I braided the strands into two chunky plaits that dangled down to my shoulders.

Opening the bathroom door, I spotted the pile of folded clothes on the bed. I exited the bathroom and strode into the bedroom. Quickly pulling the huge T-shirt over my head, I stepped into the sweatpants, dragging them up to my waist. Even after I tightened the pants' drawstring and rolled up the legs, they hung baggy around my ankles and rode so low on my hips they threatened to slide down, revealing my bare ass. Frustrated, I yanked them off without untying them. Thankfully Quinn's T-shirt was long enough to cover me to midthigh. I only needed to sleep in the shirt. Then in the morning, I could put my clothes back on.

Returning to the bathroom, I gathered up my clothing and boots from the floor. I needed to wash my clothes and wipe off my boots. I left the bedroom in search of Quinn.

"Feeling better?" Quinn asked, looking larger-than-life from his spot leaning against the wall across from where I exited.

"Yes, much better." I felt compelled to step forward. I'd never experienced such a quick, powerful reaction to a man before.

His eyes moved from my face, past the bundle in my arms, to my legs, making me feel naked. A tight, prickly feeling rolled over my skin.

"My head is a dull ache." I paused. "The sweatpants were too big," I informed him.

"Figured as much." Returning his gaze to my face, he said, "Let me show you my laundry room." He abruptly walked away. I had no other choice but to follow him.

He walked down to the middle of the wide hall and opened a door. "The washer and dryer are in here," he said, stepping inside and turning on the light before allowing me to enter.

He opened the white cabinet that had detergent and other supplies inside. "Take what you need."

"Thanks." Placing my clothes inside the washer, I adjusted the temperature and added the detergent to it. Once it started, I put my boots on the counter before turning to face him. His gaze was intense as he stared at me. The look made my heart rate kick up, as if I'd just run through the pasture again.

Now that I no longer had my muddy clothes in my arms, there was nothing to distract me from his seductive, sensual scent—vanilla intermixed with coffee and sandalwood—that made me want to close the gap between us, pressing my body against him.

My feet slid a few inches forward.

His nostrils flared while stepping closer, but he didn't touch me. It was as if he was waiting for me to make the first move or give him permission to touch me.

My pussy tingled, and a delicious warmth spread throughout my body. My breath heaved in and out of my lungs. His nearness sent me past arousal, into blistering lust.

I have to be out of my mind.

Part of me cautioned to step back, maintain distance, because this attraction between us didn't make a bit of sense.

What the hell am I doing?

Gathering my strength, I said, "I… um… I need to get some sleep." My words came out more forcefully than I intended, but I felt agitated, uneasy in my skin.

"Imani…"

But I'd already escaped the laundry room, striding quickly to the guest bedroom. Once inside, I locked the door. Crossing to the bed, I grabbed my cell off the nightstand. "Shit. Still no signal," I mumbled before sliding under the comforter.

As I stared out into the dark room, I prayed for morning to come soon. I had to get away from this house and Quinn before I ended up making the biggest mistake of my life… inviting Quinn into my bed and into my heart.

CHAPTER 7
IMANI

I felt refreshed and ready to start my day due to a restful night's sleep, clean clothes—thanks to using Quinn's washing machine and dryer—and a borrowed pair of sneakers from Piper.

I stood next to Quinn, and we watched the tow truck driver —his friend Emmett, who owned the only garage in town—carefully pull my vehicle away from the tree. Frankly, I'd never seen someone so skilled with a tow truck before. Reassured that my vehicle was in safe hands, I glanced around at the diverse array of flora and fauna in the woods surrounding us. The scenery looked like a rich and colorful world, waiting for me to discover it.

"In the daylight," I started, "your woods don't seem so scary."

"Actually, it's a rain forest." Quinn clarified.

"Even better," I said. "I'd love to take a walk in it." Even though I'd spent lots of time in the city, my love of nature called to me, and I always drove to neighboring woods as my adventure escape.

Quinn turned to me, frowning. "Not a good idea."

"Why?" I countered.

"Too many wild animals."

"Like that Bigfoot wolf that chased me?" I shivered just thinking about the huge mutant black wolf.

"There's no such thing as a Bigfoot wolf," he said.

"So says you." I looked him up and down. "It was dark, but before it gave chase, I swore that animal stood upright on two feet not four."

He scratched his chin. "I don't doubt that, Imani. But it was a wolf. A dangerous one. In fact, there are other wolves just like that one around. You don't want to mess with any of them."

"What about if I go out only during the day and keep to the trails?" I inquired.

"No." He shook his head. "It's better not to go at all. There are too many wild animals that don't take kindly to people wandering into their territory. It's not safe. But if you really want to go exploring through the rain forest, either my friends or I will go with you."

"Quinn, I don't need a babysitter." I jammed my hands on my hips. "I'm an experienced hiker."

Leveling his blue eyes on me, he folded his beefy arms. "This has nothing to do with you or your skill set. Like I said, it's not safe."

I knew I was unreasonable; he knew this landscape better than I did. But him telling me what to do was pissing me off.

Emmett, a tall man with dark hair pulled into a ponytail, hopped out of the tow truck, giving my car a once-over. "Looks like she's not in terrible shape, Imani. I'll have to check her out over at my shop to make sure, but if you're very lucky, your only problems will be cosmetic."

"I don't mind so much about that," I answered. "The car is something like ten years old. Just thanks for towing it out and taking it in to look at. I figure I've got enough to cover the cost as long as nothing is seriously wrong. I can't afford to replace it." I really couldn't—all my savings were in my handbag, so I'd have to be very frugal with my expenses.

"Don't you worry about that any." Emmett shook his head. "Quinn said he'd cover the cost of repairs."

I shot Quinn an incredulous stare.

He shrugged a massive shoulder. "It needs doing," he said simply.

His generosity floored me, but I couldn't accept. He'd already gone above and beyond with helping me.

"Quinn," I breathed. "Not that I'm not grateful, but I'll pay my own debts, okay?"

Quinn frowned a little but then nodded amiably enough.

I turned a smile on Emmett, who looked mildly impressed. "Emmett, just let me know how much it will cost."

Emmett nodded before I hopped into Quinn's black pickup. I was grateful that he would give me a ride into town while trailing after the tow truck with my car jacked up on its back.

"Quinn?" I started.

"Yep." He eyed me briefly before returning to the road.

"Thank you." I swallowed over the lump of emotion in my throat. He was a stranger who was doing more for me than anyone in my entire life, and that said a lot about his character.

"Anytime, Imani."

As he continued to drive, I took my mind off my problems and just enjoyed seeing the lush rain forest view.

"So how do you feel today?" Quinn rumbled at me.

"A lot better. And despite all the chaos from last night, I slept like a damn baby." It didn't hurt that my sleeping quarters looked like a five-star mountain retreat. Complete with its own stone fireplace, thick log walls, tree-trunk beams, a king-size bed, and a decadent private bath with a big soaking tub and double sinks.

I bit my bottom lip. "Frankly, it's the first decent night's sleep I've had in days. It must be the Alaskan air or all that cardio I did running away from that mutant Bigfoot last night." I shivered, just remembering its feral eyes. "But really, I just want to thank you again for letting me stay the night." Even though our initial interaction had been less than stellar.

"Not a problem. We don't get too many visitors from out of town around here. So your showing up on my doorstep was pretty rare." He eyed me briefly. "The wound on your head looks a lot better today, but I saw you're moving a little stiffly."

"My body will heal," I whispered. I was underplaying things by a lot. The bruises hurt; under my clothes, I had blue-black splotches from my shoulders to my upper thighs, and my feet and legs also had smaller bruises. Not to mention that my shoulders hurt from launching myself over the fence at top speed, though my fingers and toes seemed all right.

I can't change how much it hurts; I just have to ride this shit through. I'd mend.

"You still thinking about taking the job with my mom?" Quinn asked.

"Of course," I affirmed. "If she'll have me."

"No second thoughts after what happened with that wolf last night?"

I arched a brow. Was he trying to get rid of me? "I sort of risked everything coming here, so I've got nowhere else to go."

All true. I desperately needed this job with Piper, or I'd be jobless and homeless and looking for another place to land for the season.

I hoped that I could prove to Piper that I was the right woman for the job because, frankly, I needed the money, and I wasn't sure what I'd do if I didn't get it. I didn't have anywhere else to go—no family or friends to turn to—and I wasn't looking forward to the last resort, living in my car until I found another job and apartment.

When we reached the crest of the long, winding road, I could see the town sprawling across the middle of the valley with a body of water surrounding it. We descended onto a flat road and drove a few more minutes before reaching the section of Black Forest that seemed to be the center of activity.

"We call this Main Square," Quinn explained. "There's only one street that runs straight through it."

"It doesn't look like time has touched it." There were no streetlights, and the tree-lined street had a host of shops with rustic brick exteriors.

"That's deliberate," Quinn replied. "The town's citizens voted to eliminate traffic lights and hide any hints of modern technology. But that doesn't mean the folks here don't have cell phones and laptops—we just don't flaunt them."

"It's incredibly charming," I said while rolling down my window, allowing the warm air to brush against my face. "How many residents live in Black Forest Ridge?"

"About 773 registered townsfolk, but we have a lot more who prefer living off the grid."

It was a fair-sized town that looked as if it could accommodate at least a few hundred people. The tree-lined street was home to multiple shops, including PANTHERA ONCA FINE ART GALLERY, BESSIE'S COFFEE SHOP, a posh-looking boutique named REBELLIOUS ROSE, a brightly painted storefront with a hanging NYX'S YOGA STUDIO sign, an herbal apothecary with a handpainted window that promised HERBS, OILS, TEAS, TINCTURES, and a whole block dedicated to a warehouse storefront named SINNER + DO SMOKEHOUSE.

"Quinn," a beautiful redheaded woman called out loudly, but he didn't stop or acknowledge her.

I looked back and saw the pissed expression on the woman's face.

"Ex-friend?" I asked.

"No," he gritted out. "It's complicated."

I gave him a side-eye, storing that information for dissection later.

We drove past a few more businesses, including a tattoo parlor, coffee shop, diner, and several bars.

Most of the townsfolk looked a little eccentric. A trio of older men with shaggy gray hair loitered under a diner awning. A pregnant woman with a butt-length silver braid and a crisp white dress pushed a stroller down the sidewalk.

The entire atmosphere was weird and strangely festive, as if a bunch of cosmopolitan Berkeley hippies had taken over the town. But what was a little bizarre was that almost everyone wandering in and out of the open shops stopped in their tracks to gawk at me like I had two heads.

"Black Forest doesn't get many visitors, huh?" I asked.

"Nope," he replied gruffly. "And they like it that way."

"I don't get it." I frowned. "If this town isn't interested in tourism, why is your mother building a B and B?"

"She's convinced that the entire town is lacking in common sense, so she doesn't give a shit what they want or think."

"Do you agree with her?"

"Yep," he answered.

He drove for a bit longer before pulling up in front of an enormous building with an EMMETT'S AUTO SHOP sign on the left and a BANE'S FORGE sign on the right. "We're here." Shutting off his truck, he hopped out, barreling around the vehicle to open my door.

When I got out of the truck, pedestrians gawked, whispered, and pointed at me like I was an animal in a zoo.

"Move along," Quinn barked at them, then glanced at me. "Let's make this quick. I don't want you to be late for your interview with my mom." He started to walk away, but I grabbed his arm, stopping him.

"What's going on, Quinn? Why is everyone acting so weird around me?"

"Don't worry about it. You'll be fine. Just don't wander off by yourself until I sort out some stuff."

I glared at him because his words sounded ominous as hell.

He ignored my stare and walked away.

I followed him inside a small waiting area that was empty. Quinn started striding toward the back, but I grabbed his arm again.

"I know when a person is trying to avoid a subject, Quinn." Especially since I was the queen of avoidance. "But I will not press you on the level of drama my presence may or may not cause in Black Forest because you and Piper have shown me a lot of respect." I looked him up and down. "But if there's some shady shit going down that might endanger my life and well-being, give me that damn heads-up right now." I tapped my feet, waiting for his response.

He stared at me for a few seconds. "This is a real small town, Imani. Most residents don't like change, and you being here is a change."

I clenched my fists. "Maybe coming here was a big mistake."

He stepped closer.

"More like destiny," he answered in a raspy voice. He reached his hand forward, touching my cheek.

His eyes searched mine, as if daring me to make the first move.

I reached up, sliding a hand up his chest to his shoulders, feeling his muscles bunch through the material of his shirt.

He let out that low, contented rumble.

"You little shit, come back here with that!" Emmett's irritated voice yelled from another area in the auto shop.

We both glanced over toward the ruckus.

"Jacob." Emmett's deep voice rang loud as it drew nearer. I could hear the thump of his boots and something clinking and pattering.

A moment later, a ferret with dark eyes, a pink nose, brown mask, and white chin came squiggling into the waiting area, running fast with a large, shiny hex wrench in its teeth. The animal chittered around the steel, sounding almost like it was giggling.

"Oh hell." Quinn moved to intercept the creature. "Jacob! Dammit, drop the wrench. Emmett has a car to fix."

They named the ferret Jacob?

I stared at the furry creature that had a cone-shaped nose,

thin tail, and a long, pear-shaped body with short legs and long claws.

Is it normal for a ferret to be so big?

Then I remembered the giant wolf from last night. Did they just grow animals bigger in Alaska?

Quinn chased the dodging, chittering creature around the waiting area.

Emmett came in and started doing the same, swearing under his breath the entire time.

The ferret almost escaped with the wrench, but I darted forward and slammed the front door in its face.

The ferret plowed into the door with a thud and somersaulted backward, its form blurring and shifting as it tumbled, until a skinny, nude, stripey-haired boy landed on the floor where the ferret had been.

What the hell just happened? A wave of fear and confusion washed over me.

With mischievous eyes, the boy looked between Quinn and Emmett, who were standing over him.

The gangly boy stood, grinned, and handed over the wrench. "Hey, you looked like you needed a break," he said in a slightly high-pitched voice.

Emmett scowled down at him, snatching the wrench away.

"Fucked-up timing, Jacob," Emmett grumbled, and then he looked over at me, as did Quinn.

I stared at the boy who had been a ferret just a moment before. My brain kept trying to tell me that what I had just seen was impossible, but I knew it had been real.

Jacob stared back at me, sniffing the air loudly. "Wait, she's a hybrid?" His jaw dropped.

Quinn looked between the ferret boy and me.

"Shit," Quinn muttered.

CHAPTER 8
QUINN

I stared into Imani's shocked eyes and sighed, hunting around for the right words. "Sorry you had to see that, Imani."

Jacob started edging toward the door again. "Don't move," Emmett warned him.

"This little jackass always thinks it's funny to mess with people trying to get things done around here," I explained.

"Hey, that's not fair." Jacob pouted.

I lifted an eyebrow, and he shrank a little.

Tell her everything. She will learn anyway, my inner wolf suggested.

It is too soon, I replied to my beast.

But I also knew that Imani wasn't about to let what she saw go.

My wolf snorted. *And when will you tell her that she is our mate? Ours to love and protect? The female who will keep us from going crazy?*

When I'm sure she's ready to accept that she's mine, I answered.

As far as I was concerned, finding out that she was a hybrid would be shocking enough. But the knowledge that she was the mate of an alpha wolf-shifter might send her running out of town, rejecting me altogether without giving me a chance to prove that I was a worthy mate.

Imani blinked slowly and gaped between Emmett, Jacob, and me, then closed her eyes, taking a few deep breaths. Once some tension left her body, she opened her eyes, narrowing them on me. "Quinn, what the fuck is going on?" she demanded.

"I know this has to be a shock, but just trust me. There's no need to panic."

She scowled. "I'm not panicking. Ferret Boy is about as intimidating as a kitten."

"Hey," Jacob grumbled. "That's not very nice, lady."

I snorted. Emmett stifled a chuckle.

She gave Jacob an unimpressed stare. "Well, it's true."

"You're not freaking out," I observed, watching her face. "Not really anyway."

I could see her pulse beating hard in her neck. Her eyes were wide, and I could smell the stress pouring from her body. But strangely, Imani wasn't screaming, running, or blabbering words of denial. In fact, she was taking this whole thing damn well so far, considering the situation.

"I'm not losing my shit because I'm in shock," she admitted, rubbing the back of her neck while pacing back and forth. "Butt-naked Ferret Boy"—her voice rose as she jabbed a finger at Jacob —"just broke the laws of physics in front of me." She stopped, turning to eye all of us. "And I don't know what to make of all this crap."

I rubbed my jaw. "Yeah, about that. Look, like I told you earlier, we don't get many outsiders around here, so I'm not exactly used to having to explain all this to a hybrid."

"Outsiders?" she exclaimed. "Hybrid?"

I glared at Jacob and then eyed Emmett. "Do me a favor and escort this petty thief back out. Huh, bro?"

Emmett nodded.

I gave the ferret-shifter a hard stare. "As for you, go home.

And don't mess with Emmett again while he's working, or it's my boot up your ass. Got it?"

Jacob nodded, a little wide-eyed, and glanced at Imani briefly before hurrying back toward the garage.

Emmett and I exchanged a quick glance before he said, "We've got fifteen minutes, tops, before Jacob goes snitching to his grandmother about Imani."

"I know," I agreed.

Even though Jacob was only ten years old, he had the biggest mouth in town. It wouldn't take long before he told his grandmother, Gertrude—a member of the town council and the leader of the ferret-shifters—about Imani's presence, if someone hadn't snitched already.

"Okay. Well, let's get to sorting out this mess. Fast," Emmett grumbled before ushering Jacob into the garage.

"Imani." I rubbed the bridge of my nose. "You've already had a hell of a night. I really wanted to ease you into this."

"This?" She sliced a hand through the air. "Quinn, cut the bullshit. No dancing around whatever is going on. Out with it." Her brow wrinkled.

"It's complicated," I barked.

She skidded to a stop. "I'm in a town that isn't on any map. I got my car knocked out of commission by a Vegas-like light show, then I was chased down by a gigantic, crazed wolf. Everyone in town who's seen me has glowered at me like I'm some intergalactic alien that just landed in Black Forest. And now this shit with Ferret Boy." She swallowed hard, still keeping admirable control but clearly unnerved. "So don't even think about sugarcoating shit. Just rip the fucking Band-Aid off and give me the damn truth." She studied me. "Right now."

I watched Imani for a solid minute.

"Okay, Imani." I heaved a sigh. "There's a reason Black Forest Ridge isn't on any map. There's also a valid explanation for why everyone's shocked as hell to see you here." I ran a hand over my hair before I dropped the truth bomb. "Humans and hybrids don't know this town exists."

Imani put a fist on her curvy hip and tapped a foot. "Well, I'm human, and I'm here."

"You're a hybrid—half-human, half-shifter. I can smell it." I tapped my nose. "All of us can. That's why everyone was acting so strangely around you. We shifters have acute senses—sight, smell, hearing, taste, and touch."

She looked me up and down. "You look pretty human to me."

"Shifters have two forms—human and beast. But I am not a human. And neither are you," I finished pointedly.

She frowned. "Why do you need a human form? Why don't you just be… you know, a beast and live in the wild?"

"Just like cavemen, we've evolved." I didn't mention that the unmated male population was going backward in terms of evolution due to the feral sickness. "Shifters live among humans, but there are some who choose not to, like the residents of this town that is hidden by a magical veil."

"Magical?" She blinked, then blinked again.

"Yes."

She frowned. "Okay, I'm not going down that magical rabbit hole—for now. Let's get back to the topic of hybrids. You claim that I'm a hybrid, and from the side-eyes I've received from everyone, I assume we are not welcomed here. Why?"

"All the shifters in this town, including me, are considered full-blood." He paused. "Even the vampires."

"Vampires are real?" she squeaked.

"Yes," I replied.

"But…"

"Please, Imani, let me finish."

She nodded.

I continued, "They're unwelcoming because you're not of full-blood. And they consider hybrids to be weak."

She arched a brow. "Is that what you believe too?"

"No," I answered truthfully, but I was in the minority.

"So I'm assuming my human blood is what makes me weak in their eyes."

"Yes. Hybrids are created when a shifter—and his or her—human fated mate have unprotected sex."

Her eyes widened.

"In essence," I continued, "shifters can only procreate with their fated mate."

"And what is a fated mate?"

"A soul mate," I answered.

"Soul mate?" She snorted. "There is no such thing."

"I beg to differ, Imani. Shifters are only deeply connected to their fated mate."

"You mean deeply connected in a dependent or needy way?" Distrust glittered in her eyes. "You shifters sound like some sort of cult."

"We are not a cult. We are a race of beings that believe there is one shifter—our fated mate—whom we were born to love."

She rolled her eyes. "People confuse love with lust all the time."

Her words confirmed what I suspected—I would have a hell of a fight coming my way trying to convince her that she was my fated mate and she belonged to me. And I to her.

"Darling, are you confused about the difference between love and lust?"

She stared at me boldly. "Nope. I've been in lust lots of times. That's why I'm still single."

I stepped forward, tracing a finger across her cheek. "You've been in lust but not in love." It was a statement, not a question.

"That's none of your business." She inched back from me.

"So that's a no," I said dryly.

"No, that's personal." She glared at me. "Let's get back on topic, shall we?"

I shrugged. "I thought we were on topic."

"No. We are most certainly not." She moved farther away from me. "If I'm a hybrid, why haven't I shifted?"

"Because you haven't met your fated mate." *Me*, I left unsaid. "When you do, your inner animal will start to awaken. Your senses—sight, smell, hearing, taste, and touch—will start to heighten. Also you might be able to shift into your animal."

She pointed a finger at me. "Don't sign me up for shifting."

"It could happen." If she accepted me as her mate, her ability to shift would go a long way toward townsfolk accepting her as alpha female of this town. Not that her shifting was a prerequisite for claiming her.

She crossed her arms. "Not if I don't meet my 'fated mate.'" She made air quotes.

I stepped closer. "Too late, darling…" I growled. "You already have."

"Who?" She snapped, backing away.

"Me."

She gulped. "But how could you know that?"

I tapped my nose. "I scented you the moment I opened my door. Shifters know our mate by their distinctive scent."

"Are you saying that I smell?"

Inhaling deeply, I said, "Your scent is alluring to me. There is no denying your unmistakable scent. You are my fated mate. The woman I've waited a lifetime for."

She pursed her lips. "What you're feeling is lust."

"It's not lust." I wrapped an arm around her waist, tugging her against me. "I want to love and protect you."

"And fuck me."

"Yes," I admitted. "That too. I won't apologize for wanting to strip you bare so that I can worship your body like the beautiful, strong goddess you are. With my tongue, hands, and cock… until we are exhausted and our scents are all over each other."

I could now smell the sweet scent of her arousal. It was intoxicating. My cock thickened, and I knew she could feel it pressing against her stomach. I wanted her to know what she did to me.

"That's not going to happen, Quinn. I'm here for a job, not for a relationship."

Her rejection was like a punch to the gut, but I brushed it off because I suspected her words were coming from a place of distrust and fear.

"Imani, I want more than a fuck," I confessed. "I want your love. Your trust." I released her. "But I know it will take time to earn both."

"Quinn, you seem like a great guy, but I'm not your fated mate. I don't know shit about love. And frankly, I'm not interested in a relationship with you or anyone else. I'm here to do a job and then move on. That's why I answered your mother's job posting."

"There is no job posting," I said bluntly.

Her mouth fell open, then snapped shut. "You mean she's no longer hiring?"

"She has a bed-and-breakfast she's opening," I explained. "And she will need a chef. But she didn't put any ad online, and she didn't talk to you over the phone."

"Bullshit." She reached into her enormous bag, quickly fumbling inside before pulling out her cell. Her brows knitted while she swiped a finger across the screen. "But I had the driving instructions," she croaked while she searched her device. "I noted it and a copy of the ad. Shit. Why can't I find it? Fuck! What's the area code here?"

"Nine zero seven. That's most of Alaska." My voice was calm as I watched her quickly scroll through her cell and become visibly frantic when she couldn't find what she was searching for.

My inner beast whined, sensing her discomfort. I also felt uneasy watching Imani.

I wanted to pull her into my arms, protecting her, telling her everything would be all right. But I knew that would do more harm than good. Imani had to come to terms with this situation on her own, or she'd always question whether everything she'd just heard and seen was true or a figment of her imagination.

"Nothing," she hissed. "My cell is saying that I've never called or taken a call from anyone in that area code." A sheen of sweat appeared on her cheeks, chin, and forehead. She fanned herself with her hand.

Oh damn. She's about to blow.

Rushing over, I grabbed her hand, stilling her agitated movements. Rubbing a thumb over her skin, I felt her calm instantly.

My wolf came so close to the surface, I could feel the brush of fur just beneath my skin.

I dislike this, he grumped. *It hurts to see her suffer like this.* I silently agreed.

"This is crazy," she rasped, her eyes locked with mine. "What about the notes I took?" She yanked her hand away, fingers trembling as she started swiping through her cell again. Not finding what she wanted, she looked up at me in shock. "But how can I have memories of a phone call that doesn't exist? And of taking notes that aren't on my cell?"

Muscles jumped under her skin. "Quinn, I'm not crazy. I swear I didn't make this shit up. What the fuck is going on?" she shouted.

"I believe that you were called by Freya's spell."

"What?"

"Long story short, a year ago, Freya cast a spell calling the fated mates of all unmated Ridge males."

"Mating spell? Witch?" She blew out tiredly. "You sound batshit crazy."

"But deep down inside, you know I'm telling you the truth." I locked eyes with her.

Imani sighed. "Continue."

"Freya's a powerful witch," I explained. "And the head of the town's witch coven. I'll bring you to meet her."

"Nope. Not happening. I'm not interested in meeting a witch. What if she tries to put another mojo spell on me?"

"There's nothing to fear, Imani. She's a good person, my mother's best friend, and I've known her my entire life. Besides, you have to meet her. She needs to confirm what my gut is telling me—that her spell brought you to the Ridge."

She tilted her head, examining me. "Why is knowing so important?"

"Because Freya's highly respected in this town, and her official word on the matter might help calm the residents' fears about the why and how you're here. Once she confirms my suspicion, I'll also have to call a town hall meeting because—"

"Quinn, stop!" Imani yelled. "Give me a minute to process this mess." She walked over to one of the seats and lowered herself onto it.

Minutes ticked by in utter silence.

I watched as Imani sat with her back straight and eyes staring at nothing in particular for an excruciatingly long time.

"Okay, explain the mating spell thingy again," she demanded. "And this time, go real slow, like I'm a cranky two-year-old who missed her nap, because that's exactly how I feel right now."

CHAPTER 9
IMANI

I sat in Quinn's truck, staring out of his passenger window and trying hard not to beg him to drive me straight out of the Ridge and back into the human world. Leaving my out-of-commission car, along with this crazy world, behind. But a part of me thirsted to know more about this town, shifters, and me. So I agreed to meet Freya.

Quinn drove up to the Cauldron Saloon, where Piper was waiting outside for me.

He eyed me. "You okay?"

"No." I bit my lower lip. "But I'll manage." I was a little apprehensive about what else Freya might reveal.

"I would go inside with you, but I have to meet up with Rhett to figure out a plan to handle all the backlash we'll get from the residents who know you're here."

"And Rhett is?" I prompted.

"My friend, pack beta, and the town's sheriff."

"Quinn, if they don't want me here, maybe I should just leave town," I suggested.

His fingers brushed my cheek. "You can't run from destiny, Imani, and neither can they." He smiled at me. "Don't worry about it. One step at a time. You need to meet Freya."

I nodded. "Right."

He got out of the truck, opening my door. Getting out, I stared up at him. "Be safe."

He lifted my hand, kissing my fingers. "Always." Releasing my hand, he walked away, getting back into his vehicle and driving off.

Piper walked up to me. "So how are you doing?" she asked while rubbing my arm.

"A little overwhelmed."

"As it should be. From what Quinn told me, you just had a hell of a lot of information about our world dropped on you like a bomb." Piper looped her arm through mine. "Come, let's go meet Freya."

When we stepped into the empty Cauldron Saloon, it wasn't quite what I'd expected.

The establishment was more like a swanky Manhattan club than a dive bar. It had a dance floor, and the whole place was constructed from dark wood and burgundy leather, with upscale-looking lights gleaming from the ceiling and under the edges of the expansive mahogany bar. From the corner of my eye, I caught a large concert stage, and a smaller one with gleaming brass dance poles dominated the far end of the space. Spotlights stood ready to frame the now-absent dancers.

"The saloon doesn't open until later," Piper informed me. "Hey, ladies. I've brought Imani with me," she chirped at the two women sitting in a booth.

"About time," they both said.

I watched a woman with short and natural hair move out of the booth, heading toward us. I smiled when I read her black T-shirt with the slogan, WITCHES GET SHIT DONE.

"Love the shirt," I said.

"Thank you," she replied. "I'm Nyx."

"Nice to meet you, Nyx." I smiled. "I presume you own Nyx's Yoga Studio."

"Yes, I do. I have the best yoga studio in the Ridge," Nyx replied.

"Don't you mean the only yoga studio in the Ridge?" the woman she was sitting with argued.

Nyx rolled her eyes. "That's my mom, Freya." She jabbed a finger at the older woman swaying in our direction.

Instantly, I had hair envy from Freya's shampoo-commercial-worthy thick, long white tresses that contrasted sharply against her beautiful ebony-hued skin. She was fashion-runway ready, in an expensive-looking, skintight crimson sheath dress that molded to her hourglass figure.

As Freya got closer, it was her almond-shaped, whiskey-colored eyes that captured my attention. They were almost hypnotic when they focused on me. My brain got fuzzy for a second. My limbs stiffened as if being held involuntarily immobile, then my brain kicked into top gear, breaking the trance.

"That's weird," I blurted out.

Freya arched a brow. "Yes. It was."

"Freya! That's not neighborly." Piper jabbed Freya in the side.

"Ouch!" Freya gave Piper the stink eye. "Don't poke me with that bony elbow."

Piper grumbled, "Well, you know the rules. It's not polite to pulse without permission."

Freya shrugged. "I can't just turn my gifts on and off like a switch. Besides, I scan everyone I meet. It's force of habit."

"Pulse?" I asked.

"Witches like Mom and I can see a person's aura," Nyx answered. "Everyone's aura has a color. Shifters are blue. Vampires are orange. Humans are yellow. Well, you get the point. But what we can't do is tell what type of shifter an Other is unless we pulse the aura. Pretty much, it's like tapping on the glass of a fish tank, annoying the fuck out of a fish. For example, we tap on the aura to provoke the shifter's animal to reveal what they are."

Freya arched her brow. "Yes, but when I tried to pulse you,

Imani, something blocked my magic from digging further into what type of Other you are. It's as if there's a wall erected around your body, protecting you from my magic."

"Good," I replied, having no clue how and why my body did that. "Just so we're absolutely clear, I do not give you permission to pulse, scan, or mindfuck me."

With laughter in her eyes, Freya declared, "I can see you're the type that pulls no punches." She winked at me. "Don't lose that fire. You're going to need it if you choose to stick around in Black Forest." She grinned at me. "So the good news is that I can see the remnants of my spell clinging to your aura. So I know that the mating spell called you here."

I blinked, feeling my world shake. This shit was really happening.

"But you can't tell what type of shifter she is?" Piper asked.

Freya shook her head. "Nope. But her aura is definitely a hybrid shifter."

I swallowed over the lump in my throat. "I have so many follow-up questions. Like, what's Other?"

Freya stared at me a moment before she spoke. "Patience, Imani. Let's all head to the bar for some drinks." We each took a seat on a barstool while Freya poured all four of us shots of something she called BF Home Brew.

"Drink up, Imani." Nyx tapped the rim of my glass. "You look like you need it."

I took a tentative sip from my glass. The dark amber liquid burned my throat going down. "Holy hell. This shit packs a damn punch." I waited for the burning in my tummy to lessen. "What's in this Brew?"

Freya drank her shot, slamming the glass onto the bar top. "It's a special concoction that's been crafted by Brody Thorn-bern's family for years. Now he has his very own brewery and distillery in the Ridge. Others—a society of witches, vampires, shifters, and other supernatural beings—love Brew because it's the only thing that can get them drunk. Others' metabolisms churn through human alcohol like water. BF Home Brew packs a wallop."

Nyx and Piper followed suit, chugging the strong drink like it was water.

"Are you close with your parents?" Freya asked.

I took another swallow of the liquid, pulling a face as it went down my throat and hit my stomach. "I never knew my father, and my mother dumped me at a grocery store when I was ten years old."

They all blinked at me.

Piper cleared her throat before saying, "I'm sorry, Imani. We didn't know."

"How could you?" I shrugged. "Look, you three. No pity party. I survived."

Freya shook her head. "Fine, but I'm just going to say it. It's fucked up what your mother did."

"You're preaching to the choir, Freya," I agreed. "But I will not waste any mental or emotional energy over a screwed-up woman who left her child in aisle nine." I paused. "Besides, I have so many things I need to know more about, like the mating spell."

Freya grabbed something from under the bar. It was two bags, one filled with peanuts, the other pretzels.

"How about you tell us everything that led you to our fucked-up little town?" Freya asked, grabbing the pretzels and filling a couple of bowls on the bar.

Piper took the shelled peanuts, dumping them into the other bowls.

Nyx poured more shots.

I took a swallow of Brew before launching into my tale of the call with Piper, the light show, and Sam chasing me to the ranch. Once I finished, Freya, Nyx, and Piper exchanged meaningful looks.

"Come on, ladies." I peered between them. "Don't keep me in the dark."

My brows knitted when Piper told me about the problem of unmated shifter males going feral, what they also called getting the feral sickness.

Freya explained that the same thing was slowly happening in Black Forest—unmated males were gradually going feral from not finding their fated mates. That one of the feral males went to the human world, attacking humans, and his bite that was laced with the feral virus had killed the humans.

"But why don't unmated female shifters go feral?" I asked.

"No one knows," Piper admitted. "But what we do know is that unmated male shifters eventually lose touch with their human side, making them feral if they never find their fated mate. That's why Quinn asked Freya to cast the mating spell. He cares about this town. His pack. He had to do something."

Freya explained where she'd gotten the spell—a spirit—and that no one outside her coven and Quinn's pack knew what she'd done.

Freya took a sip of Brew. "I basically cast a spell that asked the universe to send the men's fated mates to them. You can describe it as an alteration of probability because that's kind of how it works. The odds shift so that no matter how improbable something is, it happens." Freya glanced at the bottle on the bar between us but didn't reach for it. "But magic is wild and willful, so I don't exactly have precise control over how the spell will manifest or the effect it will have on the women in question, or who those women will be. That part is…" Freya shrugged, her smile a little awkward.

"Controlled by fate," I interjected with words I had no clue where they'd come from.

"Yes," Freya agreed. "But most of the full-blood shifters in this town won't accept hybrids for the unmated males."

"Which is utter bullshit," I said. "And shortsighted."

"Agreed," Piper, Freya, and Nyx said in unison.

"This town seems as toxic as the human world," I spat out.

"Don't lump us all together," Piper said. "Everyone in this

room, the Bane pack, and a whole lot of Others in this town don't put up with elitist nonsense. We're only trying to lay out the facts."

"I'm a hybrid." I shifted uncomfortably. "And Quinn believes that I'm his fated mate."

"He told us." Piper grinned. "He's 100 percent sure that you're his fated mate, and I couldn't be happier for both of you."

I shook my head. "I'm going to keep it real with you. I'm a forty-year-old woman who's met far too many Mr. Wrongs. This fated-mate thing sounds like some fantasyland bullshit."

"I know exactly what you're feeling, Imani." Nyx touched my hand. "I've grown up around Others all my life and have seen some beautiful, strong, loving fated-mate relationships, like what Piper had with her mate. But when I left the Ridge to go to college in the human world, it was hard for me to reconcile the toxic relationships I'd witnessed in the human world with what I knew a fated-mate relationship to be."

I saw raw hurt in Nyx's eyes, and I knew some man had broken her heart.

Nyx carried on. "The type of love in a fated mating, that's something you have to experience firsthand to understand."

Freya touched Nyx's cheek. "Someday you will, baby girl."

I swallowed over the emotions of seeing genuine mother-daughter love.

Piper smiled at them softly before saying, "Imani, we know this is a lot to digest, but we want you to have all the facts."

"And I respect that, Piper," I asserted. "But I'm going to keep it real with all of you. I'm not interested in some long-term relationship. I came here for a job, not a love connection." I glanced at her pointedly. "A job I'm not sure I have."

"Of course you have the job," Piper said.

"You don't know if I can cook," I protested.

"Well, can you?" Piper asked.

"Yes. I've been the executive chef for several five-star restaurants."

"You're hired." Piper grinned.

"Just like that?" My eyes widened. "You trust my word? I could be a liar."

"She knows you're not," Nyx said. "Shifters can smell a lie."

"Yup," Piper added. "It smells like burned rubber."

"Well, I accept the job offer, but it's a temporary arrangement." I wanted to make my intentions perfectly clear. "I'll stay for as long as it takes to get your kitchen up and running, but after that, I'm moving on when the season changes."

Piper rubbed the bridge of her nose, another very Quinn-like gesture. "But what about Quinn?"

I didn't want to hurt her feeling, but I wasn't going to lie to her either. "If you hire me, I'll help with the B and B. Once that's up and running, I'll move on as I always do."

"You won't," Nyx quipped.

"Won't what?" I asked.

"Move on," Nyx answered.

"This is your forever home," Piper declared. "And Quinn is your mate."

"Piper—"

"Let me finish, Imani." Piper cut in.

"Fine." I shoved a couple of pretzels into my mouth and chewed.

Piper pointed at me. "The Ridge is your home now. And I know that your mating to Quinn will change this fucked-up town for the better."

"Piper!" Freya shot Piper a warning glare. "Only time will tell if that's the case."

Piper rolled her eyes. "I know, but I'm asking the universe right now to make it so."

Piper's optimism wouldn't change the reality of this situation. I was a hybrid who didn't belong in this town, but I needed to understand everything I could so I could adapt to my new reality. "Quinn said something about my inner animal awakening when I meet my mate. What's the time frame on my animal making itself… known? A day? A week? What?"

"Every hybrid is different. So I can't give you a time frame," Freya responded.

I huffed. "Great."

"But you'll know from your body's reaction," Nyx said. "Your senses will heighten."

"Your eyes will turn amber, and so will his," Freya interjected. "This is nature's sign that the mating is true."

"Yup," Piper said. "And that's when the real fun begins. The mating heat."

"What's mating heat?" I demanded.

Nyx popped a peanut into her mouth. "It's when a female is in a heightened state of arousal that only her fated mate can satisfy."

My eyes widened. "So it's a dinner bell for him to come and fuck me?"

Freya and Piper laughed.

"Imani, this is not just about sex," Freya said. "Even though shifters love to fuck."

"A lot," Piper chimed in with a waggle of her eyebrows. "But ain't nothing wrong with that shit."

"Amen," Freya said, and both of them high-fived.

"Even fifty years into my mating to Quinn's dad, he and I used to go at it like rabbits. On the kitchen counter. In the backyard. At the forge. Shit, if I even bent over to pick up a piece of paper, that man was on me like white on rice." She smiled. "Damn. Good times."

"Um…," Nyx started. "Too much information."

Piper shrugged. "I'm just telling the truth. Anyhow, once your mating heat starts, you'll be in a constant state of arousal that only your mate can quench. By the time the heat passes, you'll both be physically exhausted from going at it for days."

"Days?" I squeaked. "Like, how many?"

"It depends on the female," Freya said.

I rubbed my forehead. "Okay, I'm going to put this out there right now. No man has ever inspired that much lust from me." After fifteen minutes of typically horrible sex, I normally tapped out, booting the man out of my bed and apartment, so that I could finish the job myself with my reliable vibrator.

"Your mate will," Piper chirped.

"Are you limber?" Nyx asked with a fake serious expression. "Because if you're not, I have a yoga class that can help remedy that issue."

All three women nodded with lips curled up into a smile.

I burst out laughing at the sheer lunacy of the three. "Let's not get sidetracked, ladies."

"Too late for that," Nyx said before drinking her shot.

"Before your heat starts," Piper resumed, "during sex with your mate, his incisors will drop, and he'll bite you on the spot between your neck and shoulder. It's called the mating bite."

Mating bite? I choked on my shot, midgulp. Nyx patted my back.

"The mark shows other males that he has claimed his mate," Piper said. "That she's his to love, protect, keep happy for the rest of her life. The female also reciprocates and marks her male. The mark seals the mating bond. And for hybrids, the bite can speed up the process of them shifting into their true animal form. So that's it for the heat topic."

Freya nudged her. "You forgot about the mating ceremony."

Piper shot her a dirty look. "No, I didn't. Do you see her face? She's freaking out. Do you really want to go into all that now?"

"You should," Nyx said, pouring more shots. "Imani needs to hear it all."

Piper huffed. "Fine." She looked at me. "After the mating bite, you're not fully mated until the town witnesses the union. The town being invited is not typical, as most ceremonies are private. But since Quinn is town alpha, everyone is entitled to any invitation."

"Town alpha?" I squeaked.

Freya frowned. "He didn't tell you that he's the mayor of this town?"

I narrowed my eyes. "No. He didn't. So he's not only the leader of his pack, he's the leader of this town?"

They nodded.

"It's his job as the town alpha to keep everyone in line," Piper explained. "His great-grandfather Boris Bane discovered, bought, and developed this land that became Black Forest Ridge. Boris was the first Ridge alpha, aka mayor of the Ridge." She paused. "Generations later, the mantle passed to Quinn's grandfather, then to his dad. Now Quinn is the fourth Bane to be Ridge alpha."

Given his position, there was even more reason that Quinn and I shouldn't be together, but I kept silent on that topic and said, "Can we go back to the mating ceremony?"

"It's like a wedding," Nyx said, chomping on a pretzel. "Except instead of rings being exchanged, your mate will bite you in front of the town, and then you'll get naked in the forest and have freaky, naughty sex."

"Not happening," I interjected.

"It has to," Piper said. "That's the only way the town will acknowledge and respect your mating."

"Nope." I shook my head. "I'm not an exhibitionist, so there's no way I'd be able to do that."

Freya laughed. "It's amazing the things you'll do for the right man."

"Ain't that the truth," Piper added. "When I met Quinn's father, I knew he was mine to love for the rest of my life. Ditto for him." A deep sadness overtook her features. "When he died, it felt like it ripped my heart in half."

"I'm sorry," I whispered, hating to see the pained expression on her face.

"It's okay." She patted my hand. "I just want all the unmated males in this town to have that kind of love and happiness." She looked at me pointedly. "Including my son."

"Agreed," Freya said. "I'm not going to lie. When he asked me to cast the spell, I resisted. But I'm happy I did. Despite the repercussions." Freya and Piper clinked their glasses together.

"Fuck the town council," Piper snapped before taking a sip.

"Hear! Hear!" Nyx cried.

"The council sounds like pretty important people. Doesn't their approval make a difference whether I can stay here and work?" I countered.

"No," Piper responded. "Quinn has the final say."

"True, but there are two members—Shane and Gertrude—we need to watch carefully," Freya said. "They both have a strong base of supporters that, with one phone call, can stir up a hornet's nest of trouble for Quinn."

Popping a peanut into my mouth, I waited for one of them to elaborate.

"The town council are nine alphas, each highly respected leaders of their kind," Nyx explained before grabbing a handful of peanuts. "The wolf-shifter brothers, Wilder and Hugo, are wolves."

Piper shook her head. "They don't count. They never vote or show up for council meetings."

"But they each have a vote," Freya stressed.

Piper rolled her eyes. "Those pompous assholes don't care what happens outside of their territory."

"Will you let me continue?" Nyx said.

Piper and Freya waved a hand at her.

"As I was saying," Nyx said, "there are the alpha brothers. Bonnie, a jaguar. Isabella, a dragon. Shane, the alpha of the honey badgers. Gertrude, the leader of the ferret-shifters. My mom, the head of the witch coven. Atticus, the leader of the vampire coven. And last but not least, Quinn, the alpha of the Bane pack."

Piper jumped in. "The town council are like figureheads within the Ridge. As town alpha, Quinn has the final say about what happens in town. But in order to stamp out any uprisings, we need a majority vote by the council, allowing you, a hybrid, to stay here."

"It's more symbolic," Freya said.

"Exactly," Piper agreed. "This vote will also pave the way for any other hybrids who answer Freya's mating spell."

I frowned. "And you think this vote will be in my favor?"

All three nodded.

"That's our plan." Freya took a sip of Brew. "Bonnie, Isabella, and I have Quinn's back, no matter what. Atticus, he's the wild card."

"That's for sure," Nyx said.

"If it all goes according to plan, Gertrude and Shane will push for a town hall meeting, and once that happens, Quinn can call for a vote."

"And what if you don't get a majority vote for me to stay?" I asked, popping a pretzel into my mouth, contemplating having to leave town to search for another job.

"We will." Piper gave me a thumbs-up.

"Uh-huh." I just stared at them. They resigned me to the fact that this place had its own internal logic, even if none of it actually seemed plausible.

A cell pinged. "That's me," Nyx announced, swiping her phone's screen. "It's a text from Bessie. She says Gertrude and Shane are at the coffee shop getting rowdy with Quinn over Imani being here."

"Those two assholes are so predictable," Piper remarked.

"Yup," Freya agreed.

Nyx continued to scroll. "Bonnie and Isabella are there too." She paused. "And of course, Wilder, Hugo, and Atticus aren't there."

Freya rolled her eyes. "At least they're consistent. The three of them don't give a shit about anything unless it involves them directly."

"Ain't that the truth," Nyx said, still scrolling through her texts.

"Forget about them," Piper snapped. "I feel like marching right over to the coffee shop and setting Gertrude's and Shane's asses straight."

"No, Piper," Freya said calmly. "Let's stick to our plan."

"You're right." Piper blew out a breath. "But they're fuckers," she grumbled.

"Now we wait," Freya said.

"For what?" I asked.

"Quinn," Nyx said. "He should come over here shortly to discuss the council's demands—a town hall meeting."

"With all due respect, you three are batshit crazy," I commented.

"You're just figuring that out now?" Nyx countered.

"No. I'm just verbalizing it aloud," I responded. "Freya, slide that bottle of Brew over. Something tells me I'll need all the liquid courage I can get today."

Freya pushed the bottle toward me. "Here you go."

I poured and drank back-to-back shots while listening to Freya discussing her business trip to find male exotic dancers.

"Nyx, you missed it. There was a sexy incubus that just killed it on the pole last night." Freya fanned herself.

"Incubuses suck, literally," Nyx drawled.

"Yes, they do," Freya said with a saucy waggle of her brows. "I don't give a shit that he feeds on lust because he was hot and fantastically limber."

I couldn't help myself. I burst out laughing. They were funny.

"Honey," Piper said, "I hope that Mr. Hot and Limber is hung and into witches because you, my friend, desperately need to get laid ASAP."

"That's the damn truth," Freya chirped before clinking her glass with Piper's. "Nyx, you think he'd volunteer?"

Nyx snorted. "Probably." Then she eyed me with a twinkle of laughter in her eyes. "It's just sad that my mother has had more sex this month than I've had in years."

"Damn right I have," Freya replied.

Nyx rolled her eyes at Freya before strolling over to a wall with buttons. She pressed a finger against one, causing a low hum of music to float through the club. Nyx strolled over to the middle of the dance floor and started dancing as if she didn't have a care in the world.

Between the amusing chatter between Piper and Freya and the sight of Nyx dancing like she was on the set of a music video, I decided that since I was already a part of their three-ring circus, I might as well enjoy the fun.

"Hey, that's my jam," I called before hopping off my stool on unsteady legs and striding over to Nyx to dance my stress away.

CHAPTER 10
QUINN

When I entered Bessie's Coffee Shop, the chatter skidded to a stop, and eyes zeroed on me.

"Howdy, Town Alpha." Old Man Henry greeted me from his stool by the central counter.

"Hello," I replied.

Several customers tipped their heads to me with respect as I made my way to the corner booth where Rhett was sitting. I slid into the seat across from him. "What did I miss?"

Rhett eyed me. "Everyone knows about Imani."

My eyes shifted around the crowded coffee shop. "It was just a matter of time."

Bessie, the owner of this coffee shop, sauntered up to our booth with a gigantic smile.

"Hi, Quinn." She turned to Rhett. "Sheriff."

"Hi, Bessie," we both returned the greeting.

"It's awful busy today," I noted.

She nodded. "Yes. It is, and I don't like it."

"Why?" Rhett asked.

"Something's coming," she answered. "And it feels like trouble."

Bessie was a powerful witch and a member of Freya's coven.

So I wanted to ask for more details—like if she'd had a premonition—but there were just too many ears pretending they weren't listening to our conversation.

"I'll have a large coffee, black," I ordered. "What's the pie of the day?"

"Cheddar apple pear."

"I'll have a slice," I replied.

She eyed Rhett. "And for you?"

"I'll have the same."

"On it." She winked at us before moving toward the kitchen.

Rhett frowned while drumming his fingers on the table.

"Quit it," I barked.

Everyone snapped their heads around to stare at us.

"Mind your business, people," Bessie ordered while coming back to our table with two cups of coffee and enormous slices of pie. "Here you go." She placed our orders in front of us and then walked away to tend to other customers.

Wasting no time, Rhett and I dug into our pie.

"Dang good pie," Rhett mumbled.

"Yup." There was nothing like the delicious combination of apples and pears, paired with sharp, salty cheddar, which was complemented by the smoky hit of bacon in the buttery crust.

Mack, the deputy sheriff and pack enforcer, entered the coffee shop, marching right over to us. "The council is coming." The calm expression on his face never faltered. "They want to talk to you."

I put down my fork, irritated with the council for ruining a perfectly good pie moment.

"Give us the word." Rhett directed his words to me. "And we'll put a stop to their bullshit."

I drew in a deep, steadying breath. "No. Let them come." I would have to face the council sometime, and now was as good a time as any.

Rhett and Mack both nodded.

The door banged open. The town council filed in one by one. All conversation in the shop ceased.

The town council headed straight over to our booth. Bonnie, a jaguar-shifter, led the way. Followed by Isabella, a dragon, then Shane, the alpha of the honey badgers, and Gertrude, the leader of the ferret-shifters, was last, dragging her grandson Jacob along. Four members were missing. Freya, the head of the witch coven, Atticus, the leader of the vampire coven, and the two wolf-shifter brothers—Wilder and Hugo.

"Ladies. Gentlemen." I greeted the council. Gertrude and Shane had scowls on their faces. The remaining members wore neutral expressions. "Pull up a chair," I said.

Gertrude and Shane ignored me.

Bonnie and Isabella each pulled up a chair, sitting nearby.

Gertrude shoved her grandson forward. "Jacob said there's a female hybrid in town."

Customers gasped, but from the expression on their faces, Imani's presence was no surprise.

"Did he now?" I glanced over at Jacob, who avoided eye contact, then back at Gertrude.

"Are you saying he's a liar?" Gertrude said.

The townsfolk stared at me expectantly.

"No. He's not," I replied calmly.

The entire coffee shop erupted in yelling as patrons stood, surrounding the booth.

"There are bylaws that govern us," Shane said with a pointed stare at me. "No one is above the law. Hybrids are not allowed in Black Forest."

"Perhaps we should let our alpha speak?" Bonnie interjected easily, earning a glare from Shane.

Gertrude looked ready to object, but she eventually took a seat, lifting an arrogant brow at me. Shane followed suit.

"There is no written bylaw against a hybrid—" I announced.

Shane interrupted. "Most of our laws are unwritten and passed down."

"Well, that doesn't count," I said.

"I beg to differ." Gertrude challenged me snidely. "If we wanted hybrids here, then we would have allowed them residency."

They peppered the air with shouts of "That's right" and "No hybrids allowed" and "Kick the hybrid out."

My patience snapped. "Her name is Imani." My voice cracked through the air like a whip.

The area quieted.

"Remember your place, Gertrude," I stated. "This town is mine, and everyone is here because my great-grandfather allowed it. I can kick you and anyone I want out of this town just like that." I snapped my fingers. "So don't fucking push me."

Everyone stared at me with wide eyes because what I said was true.

I continued. "As for the council, I don't answer to any of you. The council was created to provide solicited advice to the alpha."

Isabella nodded. "This is true."

"Agreed," Bonnie declared. "We are only the alpha's humble advisers."

"So what?" boomed a man's voice I recognized. "We don't have the right to know why a hybrid is in our town?"

My eyes zeroed in on the voice. It was Sam, standing by the counter with a Cheshire cat smile.

"Quinn, did you invite the hybrid here?" Gertrude asked me pointedly.

Tearing my eyes away from Sam, I said with way more calm than I felt, "Yes."

Everyone started shouting. Chairs scraped against the floor as more people pressed toward my booth.

I looked over at Bonnie and Isabella, who were staring at me curiously. The two of them were my biggest supporters, along with Freya. So I knew that they'd have my back no matter what.

I stood up. "My decision was in the best interest of this town."

"Do you think Gertrude and I are fools?" Shane challenged.

"Is that a trick question?" Bonnie asked.

Isabella gave Bonnie a high five. "Good one."

Shane glared at both of them.

"If a hybrid can get through the veil, then so can a human," Gertrude argued.

"Is the veil broken?" Shane challenged.

"She's a hybrid shifter, Shane," I snapped. "Common sense could tell you that she got through the veil due to her shifter blood."

"Exactly," Isabella agreed. "So there's nothing wrong with the veil."

"Only Freya can confirm that," Shane said.

Gertrude stood. "Jacob saw the hybrid and Piper go inside Freya's bar."

"Well, ain't you the wealth of knowledge lately," I said with narrowed eyes on Jacob.

Jacob fidgeted and avoided eye contact.

"We should all go over to the Cauldron to discuss this matter with Freya," Shane suggested.

The last thing I needed was the council running over to Freya's business, demanding answers.

"Enough," I ordered, looking directly at Shane and Gertrude.

Gertrude sputtered. "The residents of the town have the right to know what's going on."

I was done with this petty bickering.

"I agree. It's time to set the record straight. A town hall meeting will be set for tonight." I glanced over at Rhett and Mack. "Send out a group text to the residents, letting them know." The crowd parted as I stormed over to the door, exiting the coffee shop.

CHAPTER 11
QUINN

My mouth dropped open when I crossed the threshold into Freya's saloon. Mom and Freya were sitting at the bar, drinking shots and laughing like they were at happy hour. Imani and Nyx were in the middle of the dance floor, working up a sweat while dancing.

Nyx was doing some dance move that imitated a stationary runner, while simultaneously moving her fists forward and back horizontally in front of her. Imani was doing a dance move of punching her arms up to alternate sides of her body in sync to the beat.

"Well, this ain't right," I muttered. "Not right at all." I slammed the door shut, stalking over to the edge of the dance floor to glare at them.

Imani stopped right in the middle of an air punch. "Hiya, Quinn!" she slurred.

"Hi, Imani." I crossed my forearms in front of me while I stared pointedly at her. "What's going on?"

"It's a 1980s hip-hop music dance-off. I'm doing the 'Wop.' Nyx is 'the Running Man,'" she answered with a grin. "Fifty dollars goes to the dancer who can do the most 80s dance moves. I'm winning." She batted her eyelashes almost comically.

"No, you're not," Nyx said.

"You want to join?" Imani asked.

I tilted my head and studied her. "Uh, no."

"Nyx, we'll finish this dance-off later. I need to chat with my shifter."

"So I'm your shifter?" A smile twitched across my lips.

"Didn't we already establish that?" she countered, walking over to me on shaky legs and nearly tripping when she reached me.

Stepping forward, I caught her, pulling her against my chest.

I frowned down at her. "You're drunk."

She grinned up at me. "A little."

"A lot." I sighed heavily, lifting her off her feet, cradling her against my chest before striding over to my mom and Freya. When I reached the bar, I planted Imani's ass on top of the bar and swiftly stepped between her legs, preventing her from tumbling forward and taking a horrible spill.

I narrowed my eyes on Mom and Piper. "I can't believe you four are in here getting plastered while the council is at the coffee shop ready to march over with torches and pitchforks."

Mom sputtered. "We're not drunk."

Freya nodded in agreement. "We're celebrating."

"Celebrating what?" I asked.

"The mating spell invited me here," Imani exclaimed.

"Why didn't you call me?" I glared at Mom and Freya.

"Why, when we knew you were coming over here?" Mom asked.

I arched a brow. "And how would you know that?"

"Bessie texted Nyx," Freya explained.

"Well, did she tell you that Jacob told his grandmother about Imani?"

"Oh, I know Jacob," Imani announced. "He's a fairy-shifter."

"You mean ferret-shifter," Mom said.

"That's what I said," Imani replied before planting her face against my chest, snuffling. "Yummy. You smell delicious." She leaned back to stare at me with a goofy smile. "Me likey."

Freya and Mom laughed.

"This is not funny," I chastised them. "How many shots of Brew did she have?" The cocktail was a special brew that Brody and his family crafted just for Others. As opposed to regular alcohol, their powerful concoction knocked even the largest shifter on their ass, leaving them with a major hangover the next morning.

"Maybe three shots," Mom answered.

"Five," Imani said, holding up two fingers.

My eyes widened. "That's too many shots for a virgin."

"I'm not a virgin," Imani announced. She glanced over at Freya. "Why would he think that I've never had sex?"

"He means a Brew virgin," Freya explained.

"Quinn?" Imani said, reaching up to run her fingers through my hair.

I almost purred when her nails raked across my scalp. "Yes?"

"You're the sexiest man I've ever met," she confessed.

"Am I?" I asked, cupping her cheek.

"Yep," she whispered against the skin of my neck before licking her way up to my ear. My heart thumped hard in my chest.

Mom cackled.

I shot Mom a dirty glare before eyeing Imani. "Darling, after I'm done here, you're going straight to bed."

"Yay!" She wrapped her arms around my neck. "That sounds like fun, shifter," she whispered with a throaty voice that made my cock jerk. "Just so you know, it's been a while since I've had sex, so—"

I interrupted her. "Mom, one glass of wake-up juice please."

"To go," Imani added. "I'm going to Quinn's bed."

"I got it," Mom interjected before hustling behind the bar to gather the ingredients.

"Back to the council debacle," I said.

"But watching you and Imani is much more entertaining," Freya countered.

Imani started humming a song rather loudly and off-key.

I sighed heavily. "Darling?"

Imani ignored me, adding swaying to her humming.

I tried again to get her attention. "Imani?" I reached down, brushing my hand along her back.

She blinked up at me. "Yes, Quinn?"

"I'm trying to discuss something very important that might involve pitchforks and torches," I explained patiently. "Can you give me a minute to do that?"

She mimicked zipping her mouth.

I carried on. "Gertrude and Shane rounded up some council members, barged into the coffee shop, and caused a ruckus about Imani."

"Drama queens." Freya shook her head, the look on her face something close to disgust.

"Well, the drama queens won't shut up until they know what's going on. So I called for a town hall meeting to take place tonight."

"The room is spinning," Imani whispered. "Make it stop."

"I will in a minute," I promised before kissing her forehead. "What type of hybrid shifter is she?" I directed to Freya.

"Don't know," Freya replied. "Only time will tell."

Imani pinned me with a glare. "I know Muay Thai, and I'm not afraid to use it."

I quirked a brow in her direction. "Okay." I had no clue what Muay Thai—a martial art and combat sport—had to do with my current conversation.

She nodded and went back to humming.

"I'll explain everything at the town hall, Quinn," Freya said. "Not to worry." She patted my hand. "We'll have more supporters than haters when the unmated males realize that

Imani's coming here is a sign that the mating spell was successful, which means it's just a matter of time before more fated mates arrive."

"I hope so," I said. "Because a war with the townsfolk is not what we need right now."

"Exactly," Imani interjected. "That's why I'm attending tonight's dance hall."

"It's a town hall." Mom handed her a small glass of wake-up juice. "Not a dance hall."

Imani glared at Mom, then at me. "Isn't that what I just said?"

Ignoring her question, I guided the glass to her mouth. "Drink up, darling."

She wrinkled her nose. "No." She pushed it away, sloshing a little on both of us. "It stinks. What's in it?"

"You don't want to know," Freya informed her.

"You're not helping, Freya." I shot her a warning glare before eyeing Imani. "It has a lot of good stuff that will sober you up, then put you to sleep."

"I don't need it." Imani's voice was husky. "I'll take a nap after I show you some of my kinky sex moves in bed."

My cock jerked with eagerness. "Freya, a little magical help here?" I begged, taking the glass away from Imani, handing it to Mom.

"Yay. Magic." Imani clapped her hands. "Abracadabra."

Freya laughed. "I'll help, but only because I don't want to see her drunk fighting at the town hall meeting." She flicked her finger, sending a zing of magic into Imani, putting her instantly to sleep.

"Whew," Mom said. "Imani's a handful, isn't she?"

"That she is," I agreed, picking her up and heading toward the back exit.

"Where are you taking her?" Freya asked.

"To my ranch to sleep it off." I paused. "And I'll see you two troublemakers at the town hall meeting."

"Don't you mean the dance hall meeting?" they said in unison.

CHAPTER 12
IMANI

I awoke with a start, unable to suppress the moan of pain that left my lips. I felt horrible. My head throbbed.

Memories flooded back to me.

Freya, Piper, Nyx, and me, downing shot after shot of Home Brew.

Me battling Nyx in an epic dance-off that I might or might not have won.

Quinn standing between my legs, enduring my drunken flirtatious babble.

"God, he must think I'm a complete idiot," I mumbled.

Scrambling to sit up, I tried to clear my fogged brain after my nap. Pressing my back against the upholstered headboard, I just sat there, blinking at the moonlight streaming across the massive bed. I didn't remember leaving the Cauldron, but somehow I was back in Quinn's guest bedroom.

Shoving the blanket off my fully clothed body, I scanned the room until I spotted my luggage sitting in the corner. I was grateful for the option of being able to change into a new outfit after a nice hot shower.

Someone knocked on the door.

"Come in," I called out.

The door swung open, and Nyx strode in, looking fresh as a daisy.

"What voodoo shit is this?" I croaked. "You drank as much as I did, yet you look like you just stepped off a fashion runway."

"I drank a glass of this." She placed a tall glass filled with light-green liquid that looked like celery juice and a bottle of water on the nightstand. Then she dug into her jeans pocket, pulling out a folded-up piece of paper before handing it to me.

"What's this?" I mumbled, unfolding the paper.

"A note from Quinn." She winked at me before walking over to the chair by the fireplace, plopping down.

I skimmed the note. It was the password to the Black Forest private network and his cell number. Placing the note on the nightstand, I picked up the glass, sniffing the contents. The juice smelled like a compost pile.

"Ugh." I wrinkled my nose. "What is this toxic waste?" I glared at Nyx.

"Wake-up juice. I know it smells horrible, but believe me, it's a miracle worker for hangovers."

I smelled the juice again and almost gagged. "I can't get over the horrid smell."

"Drink it the Black Forest way. Chug it, then chase it with water."

I blew out before gulping the juice that had a bitter, earthy flavor that made me wince. Once the glass was empty, I opened the bottle of water, taking a sip. The water was a strange, fizzy combination of bitter and sweet.

"What type of water is this?" I demanded.

"It comes from the town's hot springs. It's an elixir. The water is touted for having medicinal properties—both for bathing and drinking."

I arched a brow. "Are you telling me that this"—I held up the bottle—"has magical healing powers?"

"Uh-huh." Nyx nodded. "Residents love it so much that we

have hot springs water fountains at lots of spots in the Ridge." She pointed a finger at me. "Go on, drink up."

I made a face before taking a sip from the bottle. The room spun for a few seconds, then stopped. The fog in my head cleared instantly. My headache was now nonexistent.

I gasped. "Holy shit! It worked."

"I told you so." She grinned.

"How did I get here?" I asked, wiping my lips with the back of my hand.

"Quinn brought you here after you passed out."

I sighed heavily. "How did two old ladies and a yoga girl drink me under the table?"

"Easy." Nyx laughed. "We're pros at drinking Home Brew. You, however, are a newbie."

"No more Home Brew for me," I muttered.

"Famous last words."

I tried to get to my feet. "Whoa!" My head swam with dizziness. I sat back down.

"Take it easy," Nyx ordered. "Drink more water."

I emptied the bottle, then asked, "Not that I'm ungrateful for you giving me the remedy to my wicked hangover, but what are you doing here?"

"Truthfully?"

I nodded.

Nyx crossed her legs. "Babysitting you. There's a town hall meeting happening in an hour, and Quinn doesn't want you here alone."

"Hm." I ran my fingers through my hair, untangling the thick coils and sorting through my memories of the bar. Then it came back to me. "The town hall is about me."

"Most definitely. Residents are pissed that you wandered into the Ridge."

"I didn't wander here. I was called here by Freya's spell." I pursed my lips.

"My mom will explain that at the meeting." Nyx's cell

pinged. She flicked her finger across the screen. "Fuck!" she hissed.

"What's wrong, Nyx?"

"Oh hell!" Nyx yelled, jumping to her feet. "I can't fucking believe them." She threw her hands in the air in obvious frustration and paced back and forth.

Scrambling off the bed, I strode over, grabbing her arm. "What's going on?"

"That text I just received was from my mom." Nyx stumbled to a stop. "She says the town council will not only be discussing you tonight, but they'll also be putting two issues to a vote. Removal of my coven as the keeper and watcher of the veil. And the removal of Quinn as town alpha."

My body tensed. "Can they do that? Remove your coven and Quinn?"

"If they have enough votes, they can try to remove my coven." Nyx's nostrils flared. "They can't remove Quinn, but they can make his job a hell of a lot harder if they make the case that he's unfit to lead the town."

I clenched and unclenched my fists. "All because of me?"

"This is beyond you, Imani. Tonight's meeting will not only decide your fate, but the fate of all fated mates who will answer the spell. You're the pioneer of change. All three of us—Mom, Piper, and me—believe that you were the first to come here not by chance but because you can weather the storm that's brewing from your presence. Whether you believe it or not, this is not just about a job. If you dig down deep inside, you know that. And if you believe Black Forest is where you belong, then I'm asking you to fight for it. Take a stance tonight."

My heart raced because her words resonated with the longing in me I'd kept buried for so long. The need for connection, friends, family, love, a home, and community.

"You want me to attend the town hall," I replied. It was a statement, not a question.

"Only if you're planning on staying here." Nyx eyed me

pointedly. "If you intend to tuck tail and run when shit gets rough, and it will, then leave town right now."

"I'm not leaving," I snapped. There was no way in hell I would abandon Freya and Quinn in their time of need. They were in trouble because of me. I had to help in any way I could. "I will not allow the council to destroy Freya and Quinn."

I stormed over to my luggage in the corner, dragging each piece to the bed.

Nyx touched my shoulder. "Imani, are you sure you want to do this?"

I locked my eyes with hers. "If we're going to be friends, know this up front. I don't do anything I don't want to do. I'm going to the meeting because I will not let some bigoted pricks who don't even know me tell me I'm not good enough just because I'm not like them." I pulled out my bag of toiletries. "I've spent my entire childhood in the foster care system, constantly feeling as if I was being tossed out like trash or returned because I was worthless, unlovable, and defective since my foster parents refused to accept me for what I am—different. Well, that shit is not happening ever again. I'm making the choice to face this new world straight on and stake my fucking claim to it."

Turning on my heel, I headed to the bathroom. "Give me thirty minutes. I need a hot shower. I look and feel like shit."

Nyx grinned. "Okay. See you downstairs." She paused. "And, Imani…"

"Yes," I answered, pausing at the bathroom threshold.

"Welcome to Black Forest."

I winked at her. "Thank you. I'm happy to be here." And I meant it.

CHAPTER 13
IMANI

Nyx turned off the main road onto a circular driveway.

"Is this where the meeting is happening?" I asked as Nyx pulled up to a two-story mansion.

"Nope. Someone we need to see lives here."

"What kind of someone?"

"King Atticus Rasputin. He's the leader of the vampire coven and a council member."

I couldn't help but feel a stab of apprehension. "Vampire? Hard pass on that shit, Nyx."

"We need his vote at tonight's town hall meeting."

"Fine," I huffed before pointing a finger at her. "But this vampire better be everything paranormal romance novels say he is. Alpha and drop-dead gorgeous, because I just don't think I can handle the disappointment of another supernatural myth gone bust."

"Oh, he's alpha, all right." She chuckled.

I arched a brow. "But is he hot?" I asked with mock seriousness.

"Very," she finished with a smirk.

We hopped out of the car, and Nyx twirled her keys around her finger as we walked toward the house. Trees surrounded us, casting huge, inky shadows that were scary. We approached the main entrance, and a pair of security cameras swiveled to focus on us.

"King Rasputin!" Nyx called. "Please let us in. There's someone I'd like you to meet."

The front door swung open. "Follow me," a tall, pale redhead ordered, then pranced away.

We both stepped into a grand entrance hall that featured an impressive marble floor design extending out from the center of the room. I peered up at the dual staircase that led down from a balcony, surrounded by gold-embellished Roman-style pillars.

The king was filthy rich.

I glanced over at Nyx. "Who is that?" I whispered, eyeing the redhead.

"From the number of bite marks on her neck, I'd say a blood concubine."

I backed up, contemplating making a beeline for the car.

Nyx grabbed my arm. "Oh no, you don't." She slammed the door, cutting off my exit.

"You're freaking me out," I hissed.

"It's okay. He won't bite hard." She smiled saucily before ushering me down the hallway.

"Not funny," I grumbled.

"In here," the redhead snapped, pointing into an open archway.

We stepped over the threshold into a magnificent room that included a spacious living and dining area with wood and stone elements. And by the fireplace, a man was seated in a massive chair covered in red velvet with a hulking black German shepherd sitting on the floor.

"Hello, Nyx." His voice was a Russian-accented rumble. "Who have you brought me?" His cold, hard sky-blue eyes inspected me. This man was both beautiful and dangerous. I inched back.

"Hello, King Rasputin," Nyx said. "Thank you for allowing us to enter your home."

His eyes narrowed. "And to what do I owe the pleasure of this visit?"

Nyx slipped an arm around me. "This is my friend, Imani Parker. I'm sure by now you've heard the rumors about a hybrid being in town."

"I have." His voice was gravelly and dark. "Both of you, have a seat."

We strode over, taking a seat on a love seat across from him. The faint scent of incense mixed with a woodsy touch of masculine cologne lingered in the air.

"Nice to meet you," I said. Nyx was right. He was handsome as hell and apparently quite at home wearing a perfectly tailored, expensive-looking three-piece suit.

His eyes bored into mine. I felt a strange sensation of pressure being wrapped around my head. Instinctively, I tore my eyes away from his.

"King!" Nyx snapped. "That is not polite. No probing of her mind."

"What is the damn deal with you people trying to mindfuck me?" I hissed.

He smirked. "Lesson number one, Imani. Never look a vampire in the eyes."

The dog yawned, displaying unusually long, sharp teeth.

"Why?" I asked.

"Most vampires can read your thoughts, and many can control your mind, making you do wicked, naughty things," he replied.

Control my mind? Just the thought made fear twist in my stomach.

"Sexual things?" I rasped.

His eyes hardened. "That's called rape, Imani, and no one in my coven would ever do that shit. The punishment for such an act is a slow and painful death by my hands."

I shuddered. *He's crazy and badass.*

The redhead sauntered in, holding a silver tray with a goblet on top. The king took the glass, then dismissed her with a wave of his hand. The woman bowed and then exited the room.

He took a sip from the goblet, sighing as if the taste satisfied him.

"King." Nyx sat forward.

He inclined his head.

Nyx continued, "There's a town hall meeting tonight, and we'd appreciate your attendance."

The king's lips curled up into a wicked smile that made me shiver. "You mean you need my vote in favor of Imani staying in town. I've already told Freya, this battle has nothing to do with my vampire coven."

His words cut through me like a knife.

"Why?" I demanded.

"Imani," Nyx hissed, giving me a warning glare.

He laughed, eyeing me. "Brave. Beautiful. I like that about you, Imani."

I recognized immediately that in order to make any headway with him, I had to push aside any fear.

"King," I started. He inclined his head for me to continue. "Has Freya explained the circumstances that led me to this town?"

He nodded. "Freya explained it all. Your background. The mating spell. That you're a hybrid. The importance of tonight's meeting and vote." He looked at me curiously. "You've lived your entire life thinking you're human. Aren't you afraid of living in a town filled with Others?"

I had to keep it real with him. "A little. But there's no going back now that I know what I am. My entire life, I've felt different. That I didn't quite fit in out there in the human world. Here I can fit in if you people just give me a damn chance. I'm not just doing this for me, but for all the women who might answer the call, coming here. Most of them might be like me, women who don't feel at home in the human world." I paused. "And if you don't give a shit about that, then just imagine the possibility that some of those women might be fated mates for the males in your coven."

"Vampires call these women blood mates," the king said, then glanced away from me as though he was bored.

Minutes ticked by before he continued. "There hasn't been a blood mate in our coven for centuries." He drummed his fingers on the arm of his chair. "Most of us have gotten used to the lack of companionship. But I acknowledge that this solitary life has also given rise to other problems that concern me."

I eyed Nyx. She shrugged.

Fine. If she won't ask, then I will. "What problems?"

"Losing our humanity, for one."

I bit my bottom lip, struggling to frame my next question without being rude.

"Imani, just ask," the king drawled.

"I didn't know that vampires had any humanity. Aren't you considered the undead?"

He uncrossed his legs, leaning forward and examining me with his eyes.

Is he going to kill me for my statement? I scooted closer to Nyx's side.

The king snapped his fingers. The redhead came back with a tray, lowering it so that the king could place his goblet on it.

"Anything else, my king?" the woman purred while pushing out her ample breasts.

"No," he answered with his eyes still on me.

The redhead pouted while bowing curtly, then striding out.

"Vampires are not the undead," the king said. "We have a DNA abnormality. The side effect of this irregularity is the need to consume blood, as well as immortality."

Emboldened, I asked, "Can you go outside in the daylight?"

"Yes. Primarily, we do not because it's easier to hunt at night."

"Vampires eat food sometimes," he continued. "Our hearts beat, granted a lot slower than yours. We breathe. But we don't sleep in coffins or turn into bats. Vampire folklore is hilariously incorrect. Vampires are an evolved race with supernatural powers. The older the vampire, the stronger his or her gifts." He paused. "And we can procreate but only with our blood mate."

"Wow." I sat back. "The movies and books got most of this vampire shit wrong."

"Yes, they did," he confirmed. "How old do you think I am?"

"You look to be in your early thirties," I answered.

He laughed. "Not even close. I'm over one hundred years old, and I've seen things you can't even imagine. But when you've lived as long as I have…" He paused. "As long as all the members of my coven have. It's hard to keep whatever humanity you have left when you don't have a blood mate to keep you grounded."

"Grounded?" I asked. "Preventing you from going feral?"

"Yes."

"Which is why it's so important that you vote tonight," Nyx chimed in.

"And how do I know that any of these females called by Freya's spell will be our blood mates?" he demanded.

"There are no guarantees, King," Nyx countered. "Just possibilities, and that's better than nothing."

"This is true." He turned to stare at the fire for an excruciatingly long time before he said, "I will attend the meeting tonight."

CHAPTER 14
QUINN

I glanced around the hall that was packed with Ridge residents.

I nodded to Brody, signaling him to bring the residents to order.

Brody rang the bell. The piercing sound sliced through the air, causing townsfolk to scramble to their seats.

The entire attitude in the room changed in an instant, leaving a cold, hushed silence. I could feel a rush of emotions sweeping through the space like the tides of the sea—from excitement to anger to uncertainty to fear.

The members of the council walked swiftly across the stage before standing rigidly in front of their seats. I strode out, and when I reached my seat, the council sat down as one. I remained standing.

I stared at the crowd. "The council would like to thank you all for coming out tonight on such short notice. We have serious business that I will address." My gaze captured and held the attention of the entire audience. "As you may have heard, we have a visitor in town."

"A hybrid!" Prudence yelled.

The crowd's reaction ranged from gasps to yelling.

"Quiet down," I barked, and the crowd went silent. "As I was saying, we have a visitor in town, and many of you are looking for answers."

Sam stepped into the aisle and shouted, "Like, why there's a hybrid in our town!"

"Her name is Imani Parker." I barely held my temper. "Not hybrid."

"Who gives a damn what her name is?" Milton, the alpha of the owl-shifters, said.

"Damn straight," Chester "the Weasel" agreed.

"All we care about is that there's some hybrid in our town," Blanche, the owner of the only gas station in town, groused.

"That's right," Josie, Milton's daughter, chimed in.

Sam grinned with all his yellowed teeth on full display. My inner beast begged for release to wipe the floor with his conniving ass, but I reined in my animal. *Now is not the time,* I told my inner beast, *but we will have our revenge on him soon.*

"Imani"—I purposely used her name while staring at the audience—"is a hybrid shifter."

The room was so silent you could hear a pin drop.

From the confused expressions on most of the residents' faces, I could tell they still didn't understand and were trying to make sense of my words. Most of the residents of the Ridge had been born and raised here. They knew nothing about the outside world. So not everyone knew about or had ever met a hybrid shifter.

To further explain, I added, "Half-human, half-shifter. Her shifter traits are dormant."

"Dormant?" Old Man Henry, a horse-shifter, shouted. "Please speak plainly, Town Alpha."

"Alpha?" June, a lioness sitting in the audience, inquired. "May I speak?"

I nodded my approval.

June stood. "Imani's abilities will be dormant until she meets her fated mate. I know this because my niece Aurora is also a hybrid lioness."

The crowd gasped with outrage.

June rounded on some members of the audience. "If any of you says one nasty thing about my niece being a hybrid, there's going to be chairs moving from me whooping your ass."

I bit back a chuckle. June was one lioness the townsfolk knew not to mess with.

Immediately, residents averted their eyes from June, who huffed before taking her seat again.

Freya walked over to me and smiled at me with motherly affection. "May I?"

I nodded briskly.

"I pulsed Imani," Freya announced to the crowd. "So I can say with one hundred percent certainty that she's a hybrid shifter."

"What type of shifter?" Gertrude challenged.

"We won't know until she meets her fated mate and her inner beast awakens," Freya responded.

"But who invited her here?" Shane inquired.

"I did," Freya exclaimed. "At the request of our town alpha. I cast a spell. It was a mating spell that invited the fated mates of all unmated males in the Ridge to come to our town."

"What? The council didn't vote on that," Shane complained.

Gertrude's expression was thunderous. "You two had no right to do something like this behind our backs."

"They had every right," Mom said, rising to her feet.

"Mom...," I started.

"No, Quinn," she replied. "Enough! You're carrying the burden by yourself, and it's unfair. You're not responsible for this feral clusterfuck." She pointed to the spectators. "They are. You're all quite content to live your life in a bubble—pretending that the feral sickness doesn't exist." She eyed them all with disdain. "You turn a blind eye every time an unmated male goes feral, disappearing into the outer Ridge. Out of sight, out of mind, I guess."

Mom's words were true. I didn't know when or how feral

males decided to seclude themselves deep in the rain forest—away from the townsfolk—but this tradition was now an expected walk of shame.

Mom continued. "Townsfolk need to stop pretending the feral sickness doesn't exist—because it does. Our unmated males are going feral, and the rate is increasing."

Unmated males in the room shifted uncomfortably in their seats.

"Quinn had no choice but to ask Freya to cast her spell," Mom said. "The spell was a last-ditch effort to save all the unmated males in this town."

A smattering of the audience either clapped or nodded with approval.

Mom took her seat.

"Freya," Bonnie said. "Have you confirmed that your mating spell brought Imani to the Ridge?"

"Yes," Freya replied. "I sensed the remnants of my spell on Imani's aurora. She was called here by me."

"Well, I see this as a success," Isabella announced.

"You've got to be joking," Shane bellowed. "How can you call a spell that's brought a hybrid here, instead of a full-blood female, a success?"

"Hybrid or full-blood, why does it matter?" Isabella asked dryly, earning a look of derision from Gertrude and a scowl from Shane. "It's ridiculous to make this a sticking point. She's the fated mate of an unmated male in this town, which means there will be one less male who will go feral."

Gertrude interjected, "This council does not accept hybrids as a solution to the feral sickness problem in this town."

"You forget yourself, Gertrude," I ground out. "The council are mere advisers. I make the decisions."

"Be easy, Alpha," Freya soothed.

Taking a deep breath, I fought the urge to release the tight leash I had on my temper.

"But she's half-human," Gertrude argued. "How do we know she won't expose us to her kind?"

"Her kind?" Bonnie asked. "She's half-shifter. That means she's our kind."

"There is too much risk!" Shane shouted.

"Who are you to determine what is too much risk?" I countered.

The town hall door opened, and a tall man dressed in black walked in. It was Atticus. My eyes widened. This was the first time Atticus had attended a council meeting.

The audience quieted.

"I've met the hybrid," Atticus announced while making his way toward the stage. "And I can assure you she means no harm to the residents of Black Forest." Walking up the stairs, then across the stage, he nodded at me, then Freya, before taking a seat next to the council. "She is also proof that Freya's spell worked."

Gertrude made an angry noise in the back of her throat but held her tongue.

"So when can we meet her?" Isabella inquired.

"As soon as I can have a vote that guarantees her safety in the Ridge," I replied. In truth, Imani was mine to protect. I didn't need help doing so, but this vote was symbolic. It would pave the way for any other hybrid who arrived in the Ridge. It was a public acknowledgment that hybrids were welcomed here, and any harm that came to them would be dealt with severely.

Suddenly, the door of the town hall burst open. I tensed when Imani and Nyx strode inside. All the unmated males sniffed loudly while rising to their feet like waves in the sea.

"Fuck!" I spat, moving to rescue Imani from potential harm.

Freya grabbed my arm. "Wait," she instructed.

"Wait for what?" I snapped, "For them to rip my"—My words were stopped short when I saw all the wide grins and flirty winks the unmated males were giving my mate.

"Hello," Imani chirped while waving like a beauty pageant contestant until she reached the bottom of the stage.

"What the fuck?" I mouthed to Nyx, who shrugged before grabbing an empty seat.

"My name is Imani Parker," Imani announced to the crowd. "Your resident hybrid shifter."

"Wowee!" Old Man Henry called out, twirling both sides of his handlebar mustache. "That hybrid is a knockout."

The men chuckled.

Henry carried on. "She's a little too young for my taste. But if she's the type of filly Freya's spell is calling, well, sign me up."

"Thank you?" Imani directed to Henry.

"Pipe down, Henry," June instructed. "You're mated."

"I've been widowed for over ten years," Henry said. "You all know that I'm on the market again."

"Anyhoo," Imani cut in, refocusing on the audience. "I've been told there is apprehension about my presence in the Ridge." She propped her hands on her curvy hips. "But I'm here to tell you that I mean you no harm."

Shifters in the room sniffed loudly, and I knew they were scenting the air for the presence of burned rubber—a sign of deception. But only the powerful scent of her crisp, clean truthfulness wafted through the space.

"While I'm here," Imani said, "I want to get to know you, and you me."

I silently approved of her willingness to learn about our town and our ways. Socializing with townsfolk would help lessen the tension around her presence in the Ridge.

My thoughts were interrupted when Logan, a cheetah and the town's butcher, approached Imani. I smelled no ill intent, so I remained where I was but stayed alert for signs of trouble.

He extended his hand to Imani. "My name is Logan."

"Hi, Logan." Imani reached out her hand, only for Logan to bring her hand up to his nose and sniff it loudly before releasing it.

"Well, that was interesting…," Imani commented.

"You're not my fated mate," he answered with a disappointed expression.

I snorted. I could have told him that. *Imani is mine.* But this was not the right time to make that announcement to the town. Imani wasn't ready to accept her role as my alpha female. She needed time, and I would give it to her.

"Have faith," Imani replied. "She will come." Then she took a seat beside Nyx.

"Now back to what I was saying," I announced before turning to eye the council. "I put forth a vote to place Imani under the council's protection. What is your vote?"

"Yes," all the council members said, except for Gertrude and Shane.

"The majority wins," Atticus declared.

The room erupted with clapping and whistling.

I glared at Sam. "I will expel anyone from this town who tries to harm Imani."

Gertrude jumped to her feet. "This is bullshit!"

"I agree with Gertrude!" Shane yelled.

"What else is new?" Isabella replied. The crowd snickered.

Shane's eyes narrowed. "As the representative for all honey badgers in this town, I say we believe that hybrids shouldn't be allowed in the Ridge."

Bonnie snorted. "Shane, stop being such a contentious asshole."

Isabella and Freya cackled.

"How dare you," Shane blubbered. "You will treat me with respect. I'll have you know that my great-grandfather—"

"Was an asshole just like you," Bonnie interrupted him.

"And the only reason that you're on this council," Isabella added, "is because your great-grandfather was drinking buddies with Boris Bane back in the day."

"You don't even have power among the badgers," Freya said.

"Ain't that the truth," Weasel proclaimed.

Heads around the room nodded in agreement.

"Well, that's going to change real soon," Shane promised.

I glared at him. "I doubt it. So keep quiet."

Shane was a conniving, lazy SOB who thrived on creating chaos just for the thrill. He'd made so many enemies among his kind that, frankly, it surprised me that he wasn't dead by now.

Shane huffed and puffed but remained silent.

"What about the two other issues?" Gertrude complained.

I shot her an annoyed glance. "Regarding Shane's and your asinine request for the removal of Freya's coven as the keeper and watcher of the veil." I swiveled my head to eye the council. "Yes for removal, or no?"

"No," all the council members responded, except Gertrude and Shane.

"The majority wins," Bonnie announced. "Freya and her coven will remain the keeper and watcher of the veil."

"And what about my request for a vote on the removal of Quinn as town alpha?" Shane asked.

I bit back a sharp retort and said instead, "You can't vote me out as town alpha. You can only challenge me for the position." Glaring at him, I continued. "Is that what you want? To challenge me? Because if you do, let's go." I was raring for a good down-and-dirty fight to release some of my pent-up anger and aggression.

Shane paled. His bottom lip quivered, and the air stank of his fear.

"Wowee, do you smell that funk?" Old Man Henry fanned in front of his face. "That's a honey badger stink bomb."

Snickers and laughter peppered the room.

"I-I'm not challenging you, Town Alpha," Shane stuttered.

"That's what I thought," I said, and then I swept my eyes across the room. "You all know me. I don't have time to play cloak-and-dagger games. If any of you want to be alpha of this town, I'll accept the alpha challenge because that's the Others' way. We fight for what's ours. We don't whine and stamp our feet like fucking babies." My eyes went from Gertrude to Shane, then stopped at Sam. "We're Others. We battle for supremacy and territory."

"That's right!" Weasel shouted.

Everyone in the room nodded in agreement.

"Why are we talking about this shit? The matter at hand is that hybrid!" Sam screamed. "I've been a resident here for years, and I have a say—"

I cut him off. "No. You. Don't. Now sit your ass down, or get the fuck out of this room."

The tide turned on Sam. All the men glared at Sam like they'd gladly toss him out.

Sam's face turned beet red with anger. "Fuck you!" He pointed at me. "Fuck all of you!" His eyes panned the space, stopping at Imani. "Filthy hybrid," he snarled before rushing out of the town hall.

"Good riddance!" Mom yelled at Sam's retreating form. There was a thunderous roar of clapping and hooting in agreement.

CHAPTER 15
IMANI

When the town hall meeting adjourned and the room cleared, Quinn approached me.

"That was crazy as hell, showing up to this meeting," he complained.

I eyed him. "That's me, crazy Imani."

He smirked. "At least you and I can agree on one thing."

"Yep." I smiled.

"It's been a long day for you. How about dinner?" he asked.

"Are you cooking? Or am I?"

He grinned. "I'm cooking."

I scrunched up my nose playfully. "Okay, but I'm supervising."

The front door slammed open, and a tall, muscular man wearing a black shirt that barely contained his biceps and jeans with a gold shield buckle hooked on his leather belt burst inside the hall. "Quinn. Trouble outside."

Quinn shook his head. "It was bound to happen." He turned to me. "Imani, stay with Rhett." Then he moved toward the door.

"Hell no!" I ran after him. I had a feeling this was about me again, and there was no way I'd leave him defending me while I cowered in the corner.

Rhett gripped my arm loosely. "Don't do it. Our pack has his back."

"And so do I." I yanked my arm away.

Striding away with Rhett on my heels, I barreled outside and saw Quinn, Freya, Piper, Nyx, some council members, and all the men who were at Quinn's house on the first night I'd met him. They were all facing off with Sam and the knot of people standing in the courtyard, chanting, "No hybrids in the Ridge." Gertrude and Shane were egging the protesters on, and I recognized a person in the mob as the woman Quinn had ignored this morning.

"Nyx," Rhett called. "I need you here with Imani."

Nyx hustled up to the top of the stairs to stand by my side. Rhett strode down the stairs to take point next to Quinn.

"I've had enough of this shit," Quinn snapped. "Sam, I challenge you."

Sam's face turned pale. "No!"

"You dare deny me my right to a challenge?" Quinn fumed, pointing in Sam's face. "Are you that much of a coward?"

The protesters backed up uneasily.

Sam's hands clenched at his sides. "You wouldn't," he croaked.

"I just did," Quinn argued. "Imani is under the council's protection, and you deliberately challenge that decision. As alpha of this town, I am enforcing our ruling. And if you and your band of idiots want to test me, let's fucking go." He tugged off his shirt.

"You're challenging me over that hybrid bitch?" Sam exploded.

"Insult her one more time and I'll rip your head off your shoulders," Quinn barked. "So are we fighting or what?"

"Fine," Sam conceded. "But we fight as humans. And the winner decides the fate of that hybrid."

"Done," Quinn agreed.

A shudder ran down my spine as I watched Rhett, Emmett, and some other men usher the crowd back. I focused on Quinn's face, but he didn't glance my way. He had eyes for only one person—Sam.

I stood tensely, watching. Piper came over, putting a comforting hand on my shoulder. I let it stay as I stared at Quinn, my heart racing with fear.

They're deciding my fate with a fight?

Quinn and Sam stepped toward each other and then waited. I was about to ask Nyx what was going on when Sam growled, lunging forward.

Quinn nailed Sam in the face with a one-two hit, then punched him in the kidney. Sam grunted, reeling from the blows. Before he could rally back, Quinn kicked him in the knee, knocking Sam to the ground. Quinn raised his foot to stomp on Sam's face, but he rolled away and staggered to his feet.

Sam went for Quinn's middle, trying to tackle him, but Quinn shook him easily.

I watched intently, trying to keep my gaze trained on Quinn, but my eyes kept going to the gang of protesters who were leaving the scene. It was as if they knew Quinn would be the victor.

Sam kneed him in the face. Quinn staggered backward.

"Quinn!" I yelled.

"Steady, Imani. Let him fight," Nyx whispered. "You're distracting him."

I glared but didn't do or say anything else. Nyx was right. Quinn needed his attention on the matter at hand.

The fight continued, but then something happened I hadn't expected.

Sam half shifted, his face morphing into a gray wolf.

Oh hell, I recognized this beast. It was the wolf that chased me last night.

His mouth clamped down on Quinn's shoulder. With a roar

that made my skin prickle, Quinn shifted fully into a wolf. Shreds of his clothes scattered to the ground.

Quinn's shift forced Sam to release him. Quinn charged Sam, causing him to fall to the ground with a loud thump. When he clamped his mouth on Sam's throat, blood splattered.

This fight was terrifying but fascinating, and something deep inside me reveled at the display of Quinn's dominance.

Sam's face shifted back to human form. "Mercy," he begged. "Quinn. Mercy."

Quinn's beast snarled. Minutes ticked by before he released Sam.

Panting, Sam rolled over onto his hands and knees before wobbling to his feet.

Everyone just stared.

With a hand pressed against his throat, Sam bolted, racing away, trailing drops of blood behind him.

My heart was in my throat when Quinn growled, his ears sticking straight up and his teeth bared. It was as if the remaining bystanders took that as their cue, and they dispersed, leaving only Quinn's friends, Piper, Nyx, and Freya.

Quinn stuck his nose in the air, sniffing loudly as if scenting the air. Turning to stare at me, he howled.

"Well, that's our cue to leave," Rhett announced. "Quinn wants alone time with Imani."

Nyx gave me a quick hug. "I'll see you tomorrow."

I nodded, watching the area quickly clear out, leaving me alone with Quinn's wolf.

"Well, okay. Let's do this," I mumbled before making my way down the stairs. I continued moving toward him.

He was larger than any wolf I'd ever seen. He was tall, even on all fours.

A little frisson of fear engulfed me.

His wolf sat on its hindquarters, watching me.

This is Quinn. I'm safe. I took a deep, calming breath and dismissed my fear.

He was beautiful but deadly.

I stopped directly before him.

The wolf huffed at me.

I remained still for a few seconds before running my fingers across his head. His inky black fur was so soft.

I smiled, stroking my fingers over his cold nose, then over his ears. He growled. I pulled my hand away, only to have him push his head more firmly against me.

I returned my fingers to his ear, watching as he tilted his head farther into my hand, and decided that was a growl of pleasure. Before long, I was on my knees, my hands buried in the thick fur of his pelt, as I peered into his eyes.

Leaning forward, I kissed the top of his head. "Quinn, you're beautiful."

He huffed again as if saying, "I know."

"But it's time for you to shift back," I said. "You promised me dinner, and it's getting late."

Gently, he nudged me with his massive head.

"What?" I asked.

He got to his legs and backed away.

I watched with fascination, the quickness of his transformation from beast to man. A few minutes later, the monstrous inky black wolf was gone, and Quinn stood in his place, gloriously naked.

I cleared my throat, fighting the urge to run my fingers across his hairless, muscled chest.

His cock jutted out proudly as he stared at me.

Jesus. It's an anaconda.

I'd seen my fair share of cocks, but Quinn's was huge and glorious.

My eyes traveled his naked length. "Impressive," I said boldly.

He laughed. "So I've been told."

"I bet you have." I gave him a saucy wink. "Now stop showing off. I'm hungry."

"For what?" He grinned.

"Food," I quipped. "Get your mind out of the gutter, shifter," I joked.

"I can't help myself when you're around." He traced a finger across my cheek. "But it is late, and you need sustenance. So let's go." He grabbed my hand, lacing his fingers through mine before ushering me toward his parked truck.

"Ah, Quinn."

"Yes."

"Not that I'm complaining, but…" I sent him a wicked smile. "Are you planning on driving home naked?"

He laughed. "No. I have a change of clothes in my truck. I'm always prepared."

"Aww, that's disappointing," I remarked, watching his cock bobbing up and down as we continued walking. "I was so looking forward to eye-fucking you during our drive back to your ranch."

He laughed. "I'm not mad at that. I'll be your eye candy anytime."

CHAPTER 16
IMANI

After my quick shower, I strolled down the rustic staircase and into the open floor plan that connected his living room space with the kitchen area. This was the first time I could take it all in without being distracted by all the crazy shit I'd seen.

"Wow." I spun around, staring at the decor of Quinn's home. It was simply stunning and was the type of house that was featured in country home design magazines. A true family home that begged to be filled with laughter, love, and happiness—something I would never have—no matter how badly I wanted it.

"Hello?" I called out.

"In here," Quinn answered.

Striding inside, I froze when I saw that not only was Quinn in the kitchen. Rhett and Emmett were sitting at the island, along with three other men I'd seen before.

Quinn's back was facing me as he stood in front of the stove, stirring something that smelled absolutely delicious. I couldn't get over what a gigantic man he was. I could have sat on one of his shoulders easily. His back rippled with muscle that pushed against his shirt, and his long, powerful thighs bulged against the fabric of his jeans.

Rhett stood. "Hello again. We haven't been properly introduced. I'm Rhett Ward, the town sheriff—aka the Protector—and pack beta." He wasn't carrying a weapon, and instead of a uniform, he wore all black with his gold shield on his belt.

Quinn turned around. His eyes zeroed in on me. My eyes scanned down his muscular body that looked rather spectacular in his black T-shirt and dark straight-leg jeans over well-worn cowboy boots.

Shit. He's all my hot, dirty cowboy sexual fantasies rolled into one hellacious package.

Rhett pointed over at the man he'd been sitting beside. "That's Mack Owen. He's my deputy and pack enforcer."

Mack saluted. He looked like an older version of Chris Hemsworth but with dark brown hair.

"You've already met me," Emmett said. Tonight his hair was pulled into a long black ponytail. "I'm also the pack's enforcer, along with Brody and Jasper."

"I'm Brody Thornbern," said an incredibly attractive man with short-cropped, military-styled black hair and gray eyes. "I'm the proud maker of the BF Home Brew that I heard you got tipsy on."

I pointed at Quinn. "Snitches get stitches."

Quinn winked at me. "Nothing is secret in the pack."

"Hi, I'm Jasper." The last man smiled, a slow lifting of perfect lips to reveal straight white teeth. "Welcome to Black Forest."

"Nice to meet you all." My lips curled into a smile before I walked over to Quinn. I peered into the big pot filled with carrots, potatoes, celery, beef tips, and broth, just to name a few things. "Your beef stew smells delicious."

"It's leftover stew I made ahead," he replied. "I'm reheating it."

The aroma was making the entire kitchen smell delicious, and I couldn't wait to dig in.

My eyes panned the gourmet kitchen fit for a professional chef. The rustic space had a ceiling made of heavily textured exposed wood beams, richly stained inset cabinet doors, and two cooking areas designed to accommodate a variety of culinary techniques.

Damn! This is my dream kitchen.

I ran my hands over the huge, L-shaped quartz island. I loved that apparently, like me, Quinn believed that the heart of the home was the kitchen. It was the one place where you would find family and friends cooking, eating, and enjoying one another's company, day in and day out. Food brought everyone together, which was the primary reason I loved cooking and this kitchen. It had lots of room for mingling, an ample island with comfortable stools for chatting with the cook, and plenty of extra seating, such as a cozy banquette, for when the meal was ready.

"Do you need help?" I asked Quinn, who was opening the oven and pulling out the large pan of big-as-my-fist biscuits.

"No. I've got it," he replied, brushing the biscuits with melted butter. Carefully taking each piece of hot, doughy goodness from the pan, he placed them onto a platter, then brought it over to the counter.

"Time to eat," Quinn announced, nudging me onto a chair at the island.

Brody started pulling out bottles of beer from the refrigerator, placing them on the counter, followed by glasses. "What would you like to drink, Imani? Beer or sparkling water?"

I recognized the expensive, limited-edition, barrel-aged beer Thornbern Elysium. "Wait a minute. You also own the brewery that makes this beer?"

"Guilty." He winked at me.

I stared at him with amazement. "I read an article about your beer. It was touted as the most expensive beer that has been released in recent years." I stared at the bottles he placed on the counter. "They said you can't even get your hands on this beer. And if you do, you would have to pay twice the original price." Some were holding on to it, hoping to resell it for double what they paid.

"I own Thornbern Brewstillery," he revealed. "My family crafted Home Brew years ago, and when I took over the business, I added Thornbern Elysium to the product line."

Emmett nudged him. "Oh, stop showing off."

"I'll drink the beer," I said, eager to taste it.

The men washed their hands before shuffling around the kitchen, grabbing gigantic bowls and spoons, and then helping themselves to the stew before eating.

Quinn filled two bowls with stew before placing one in front of me and the other right beside it.

I stared at the massive bowls that held at least two servings of stew. "I can't possibly eat all this," I protested quietly, staring at the heaping bowl that smelled absolutely delicious. "This won't just break my diet. It will destroy it for the foreseeable future."

He took a seat next to me. "Why the hell do you need to diet?" he asked in a low and gravelly voice.

I stared at him, speechless. *Is this dude for real?*

Quinn reached out one giant hand and swallowed mine whole in his grip. His touch was scorching, and his hands were rough and callused. "Eat, darling." His warm lips kissed my fingers one by one. My body declared a mutiny, and my cunt pulsed with need.

Pulling my hand away, I grabbed a biscuit, smearing it with butter. As I took a bite, I groaned in ecstasy. The bread was warm and flaky, and the honey-sweetened butter added another layer of decadence. *Lovely.* I chewed slowly and swallowed.

"Good?" He was watching me closely.

"It's freaking yummy." I took another bite, chewing with gusto.

With a self-satisfied smile, he grabbed a biscuit, added lots of butter, and started eating. Frankly, it was refreshing to meet a man who was into actual food and not obsessed with zero-fat everything—including women—like most of the men I knew.

"These are by far the best store-bought biscuits I've ever eaten," I added.

He choked and then swallowed. "Store-bought?" He looked offended. "Darling, I made them from scratch."

Good Lord! He can make biscuits from scratch? Man jackpot!

I swallowed and stared at him. "Where did you learn to make biscuits?"

He leaned forward. "I'd tell you, but then I'd have to kill you." His face was serious, then he broke out with a grin.

I laughed huskily. "Gotcha. I don't have the security clearance to know."

"Go on and eat." He pointed to my bowl. "Your stew is getting cold."

I dug my spoon into my massive bowl of beef stew, then popped it in my mouth and chewed experimentally. I moaned softly. "Lordy. This is good too." The stew had tender chunks of meat, fresh-tasting vegetables, and diced potatoes in a thick, rich, mouthwatering gravy.

"My mom taught me how to bake and cook," he said before setting to work on his own meal. "For most male shifters, providing food for our women and young is both a duty and a privilege. Nothing is better than keeping your woman satisfied." His smile was slow and blatantly sexual, as if he was contemplating how he could satisfy me.

A flush of heat licked my skin just seeing that wickedly sensual smile. I pushed down the impulse to do something stupid, like grab his face and kiss him hungrily.

"In every way," Emmett finished for him with a suggestive waggle of his eyebrows.

Brody snorted. "Way to go, Emmett. You just ruined a sexy moment between them."

"I was being informative," Emmett complained. "You know, making conversation during dinner. Females like that." He eyed me. "Don't they, Imani?"

"I guess so," I replied before taking a few more bites while glancing around at the rest of the men who were busy shoveling stew and bread into their mouths.

"Unlike me," Emmett continued, "none of you know shit about carrying on polite conversation with a beautiful woman over a good meal."

Mack scoffed. "And neither do you. When's the last time you were on a date?"

Emmett puffed out his chest. "I watch reality shows. I've seen what the ladies like."

I laughed. "I hate to break it to you, but that's not what most women like."

They all stopped eating and stared at me with rapt attention.

"What do they want?" Quinn asked while pouring beer into my glass.

"Is that a serious question?" I replied.

"Yes," he answered. "We've all been off the dating market for years. So we're out of practice."

I frowned as we stared at each other for a few beats. He was handsome and built like a freaking god. And I'd seen his magnificent cock. So there was no doubt in my mind that he had women lining up to get in his bed.

"Dating and being celibate are two different things," I challenged him.

His gaze never wavered from mine. "I've been back to the Ridge a little over five years, and I've slept with"—he held up one finger—"one woman. One time."

I felt a spike of jealousy that I had no business feeling.

"And you've been paying for that one time," Rhett said around a mouthful of stew.

"He sure has," Jasper said. "That's why I don't go sticking my stinger in tempting honey."

"Shut it," Quinn snapped.

"All we're saying is that you have to be careful where you dip your cock," Emmett replied before taking a swig of beer.

I couldn't help laughing at their funny but honest banter.

Quinn gave him a hard stare before adding, "What I'm trying to say is, shifters are primal. They love five things—eating, hunting, fighting, dominating, and fucking. And not necessarily in that order. But we've been there, done that. Now we're holding out for our fated mates."

"Bingo," Mack said.

I arched a brow. "Except for Quinn. Who stuck his stinger in a tempting honeypot." I held up one finger. "Just one time."

Everyone snickered except for Quinn, who drained his bottle of beer while giving me a hard stare.

"I'm just saying," I replied before eating a mouthful of stew. *There. Take that shifter.*

I swallowed before speaking again. "Since we're being so transparent… What's the deal with Sam the mutant wolf?"

They stopped eating and stared at me.

"What?" I shrugged. "I saw his wolf when he fought Quinn. It was the same animal that chased me last night."

Quinn scowled. "While I was in the military, my dad died. Sam used that opportunity to take over the Bane pack and town, violently. He also tried to take my mother as his mate, even though they're not fated mates. What was left of the Bane pack either left the Ridge or had the feral sickness." He paused. "Sam's leadership tore the Ridge apart. He instigated fights between the diverse groups in the Ridge. There was bloodshed. Shifters died. Enemies made."

"He sounds like an asshole," I commented.

"He is," Rhett said.

"Agree," Quinn remarked. "I retired from the military and came back to the Ridge. I challenged him for alpha position and won."

"Why did you have to challenge him?" I asked. "Why couldn't you just boot his ass out?"

Quinn shrugged. "It's the shifter way. Dominance is supreme. We respect strength and fighting skills. We don't have time for shit-talking. In a challenge, you fight. If you win, you cement your place as an alpha predator."

"It's the top-of-the-food-chain concept," I said.

"Exactly," Rhett said.

I took a sip of beer. "I guess that makes sense. But if Sam's no longer in charge, why is he still acting the fool?"

"Because Sam's been stirring up a hornet's nest of trouble by saying that Quinn is too young to be alpha of the Ridge," Emmett said. "That he doesn't have enough experience to keep this town safe. All of that is bullshit, of course. Quinn is former Special Ops and knows how to protect this town."

They all nodded.

"Then what's their problem?" I asked.

"Most townsfolk think our pack is an abomination," Mack said.

Quinn scowled. "I don't give a shit what Sam or the town thinks."

"We don't either," Brody chimed in. "But they don't call us the misfits for nothing."

"I happen to like our misfits nickname," Jasper said. "Ain't nothing wrong with not conforming to Other society expectations. We didn't in the military, and we don't in the Ridge."

"Misfits?" I asked, not liking that derogatory nickname.

"In the Other world," Rhett said. "It's uncommon for different species of shifters to form a pack. Just like in the military, we are misfits in the Ridge. Rhett's a jaguar-shifter. Mack is a lion. Emmett, a rhino."

I blinked. "A rhinoceros?"

Emmett puffed out his chest proudly. "Yep. Jasper is a tiger. Brody, Piper, and Quinn are wolf-shifters."

"But we're family," Quinn said. "We have one another's backs, and that's all that matters."

My heart melted a little just hearing Quinn's words.

"I agree," Mack added. "Besides, we all know Sam doesn't

have the support or the balls to take the town alpha from Quinn."

"But now with a hybrid in town," I said, "he might sway some folks to back him."

Quinn eyed me. "The council voted. It's official, you're under our protection."

"But…," I started.

"But nothing," he answered. "You're my fated mate."

"Quinn…" I tried again.

"We're not going to get into that debate," he said. "It's fact, whether you want to accept it or not. And let's be clear, I didn't have the council vote because I needed help protecting my woman." He touched my hand. "Because I don't need anyone to help me protect what's mine. The vote was symbolic. The line in the sand that I wanted everyone to know they'd better not cross or they'd risk me putting a boot up their ass."

I wasn't going to lie. After spending a lifetime as a team of one, there was something sexy about having someone care enough to have my back while in town.

Don't get wrapped up in the fairy tale of happily ever after, I warned myself. *Men disappoint. All the time.*

Deciding to move on to safer topics, I said, "You have a beautiful home."

"Thank you," Quinn said. "It was built in the early 1900s by my great-grandparents. It started out as a log cabin, then it took on a life of its own as our family grew."

"Oh, so you have lots of siblings?"

He shook his head. "No. I'm the only child, even though my parents planned for more. It just never happened. This became the pack's home. And when I came back home with these assholes"—he pointed over to the men gobbling the stew—"my mom became their unofficial mother."

"We met in the military and became friends," Jasper chimed in.

"What branch of the military?" I asked.

"We all served in the Army Special Forces," Quinn offered. "But after we retired from the military, I convinced them to make their home in the Ridge. I moved in to this house and then divided the rest of the land among my friends so they could each have their own private oasis."

"Wow," I remarked. "That's generous of you."

He shrugged. "They're my brothers."

"And we fight like siblings too," Mack said.

"Ain't that the truth," Emmett mumbled between bites of food.

"About almost everything," Brody grumbled.

"Anyway, what's mine is theirs," Quinn said. "That's how it'll always be."

His words and actions summed up the man I suspected he was—Quinn seemed loyal and generous to the people he cared for.

"So what about you? Any siblings?" His eyes never left mine as he waited for my response.

I stared at him, shifting uncomfortably.

I didn't enjoy talking about my years in the foster care system; it was a horrible time for me. But something about Quinn made me want to be as giving to him as he was to me.

"No siblings," I offered. "I grew up in the foster care system, bouncing from placement to placement."

I deliberately left out the fact that I had over fourteen placements, moving from home to home, school to school, often with no explanation. I felt like I was constantly being tossed out like trash or returned because of some defect.

"That had to be rough," he said, his eyes locked on mine. I felt stripped bare before his eyes.

I shrugged and said with forced nonchalance, "It is what it is."

I took a sip of beer, trying not to think about how many times I'd had to emotionally and mentally rethread myself after being rejected each time they moved me. I'd quickly grown an impermeable emotional shell and went into survival mode, which numbed me to the frequent disappointments and abandonments.

"How long were you in the system?" Quinn asked.

I took a deep breath before answering.

I didn't want to sound too self-pitying about my life growing up. But strangely, I trusted Quinn not to judge me. He was rough, intimidating, and his manners really needed a little work, but he didn't seem to do bullshit. He didn't say things diplomatically, but he said them honestly. Quinn was a refreshing change.

"I was ten years old when my mother abandoned me, so I remained in foster care until I turned eighteen. I received a scholarship and left for college, where I got a four-year bachelor's degree in business."

I swallowed hard, remembering that every Christmas I had to leave campus, but I didn't have anywhere to go. So I paid to stay in a room the size of a guest closet. "When I graduated, I found a job in sales, so I moved around a lot—from city to city—for years. I thought my nomadic life was a phase, but I'm forty and I still have this feeling…"

He studied my face for a long minute. "About what?"

I bit my bottom lip, contemplating my next words. "Like I'm searching for something—maybe a feeling—you know, telling me that the place I'm in is 'the one.' My forever home. I know it sounds crazy, but I always get this itchy feeling as soon as I land in a new city that tells me to move the hell on."

I bit my lip when I realized I hadn't had that feeling once since I came to Black Forest.

"Anyway," I continued. "After leaving a lucrative career working in marketing and sales, I followed my passion for cooking. I didn't attend culinary school. I'm a self-taught chef, or more precisely, I learned by paying my dues in the kitchens of several well-known restaurants. My last job was at a three-star Michelin restaurant in New York."

"Sounds like a dream job. Why did you leave to come to Black Forest?" Jasper asked.

"I got the itch to move again." I shrugged. "You know, to find something new." Most people loved the stability of settling down and building a nest. I wasn't one of those individuals. I was a nomad who moved when the season changed.

"Well, you're in for a treat," Emmett interjected, "because the Ridge is like nowhere you've been before."

"Shut it," Rhett snapped, then guzzled a mouthful of beer.

"What?" Emmett asked.

Mack pushed back from the counter, picking up his bowl, utensils, and empty beer bottles. "Well, I'm done. I've got an early morning." He glanced at me. "Good night, Imani." He walked over to the dishwasher, loading it up before walking out.

"Yep, I need to get going too," Jasper said before standing. "Welcome to the Ridge, Imani."

I nodded. "Thank you." For the first time, I realized how fast they'd eaten. All of their bowls and bottles were empty.

Brody, Emmett, and Rhett each got up and wished me a good night before putting their stuff in the dishwasher and bottles in the recycling bin before walking out.

I took another long swallow of my beer, enjoying the notes of caramel, chocolate, and raisin.

"Wonderful beer," I said.

"We drink a lot of this stuff and Brew around here." Quinn flashed a brief smile.

"Where were we?" I asked.

"Why did you leave to come to Black Forest?" He stared at me, waiting for me to finish my story.

Sitting back, I sighed. "I was clicking through online job openings, and I saw your mother's job posting."

I paused for another swallow of beer, surprised by how easy it was to unburden myself to Quinn. "I took it as a sign from the universe that it was my next job, so I set up an interview meeting with her. Well, what I thought was her. And then started driving over here from New York."

His eyes widened. "That's a long drive." I could hear the

worry in his voice, and it made that warm feeling in my stomach intensify.

I shrugged. "I'm on a tight budget and couldn't afford to fly. Besides, I've traveled all over the United States in my car, but I've never been to Alaska before. It's been on my bucket list for years."

Here I was, talking to the sexiest man I've ever seen. Telling him all my business, and not once had I gotten that sick roller-coaster feeling of dread in my stomach that he'd twist my words around to break me or use me.

I glanced at Quinn, who had finished his bowl of food. I shook my head in amazement. He was all muscles.

Where did he put all that food?

He looked like a man who could take care of business in and out of the bedroom. Heat flushed through my body, just imagining how good he'd be between my legs.

Quinn's nose twitched, then his lips curled up into a panty-melting smile.

"Interesting," he said playfully.

"What's interesting?" I said, dragging my gaze away from his sensual-looking lips.

"Everything about you, Imani." He stretched my name into a sensuous whisper that slipped across my skin, leaving goose bumps in its wake.

His hand reached across the table, grasping mine. I didn't flinch or pull away as he stroked my skin. Truth was, I loved his touch. His smile. His soothing, seductive voice that made my cunt clench like it recognized its master.

I wasn't a prude, but even for me, this was way too soon even to be contemplating riding his cock like a surfboard.

Okay, girl. Breathe. Slow down.

Keep your mind off his cock.

I clamped down hard on my sexual urges, fighting the long-dormant lust unfurling inside me.

Snatching my hand away, I said, "Well, this was delicious. But it's late. I should get to bed."

"Yes, you've had a hell of a day." He stood, reaching out a hand, and I took it, rising to my feet.

"I'll help you clean up," I offered.

"Go to bed, Imani." He leaned closer. "I've got this." He backed me against the table. I swallowed hard, suppressing— barely—my surge of desire when I smelled his clean, earthy, and slightly wood-smoke-scented musk.

I cleared my throat. "I should go now."

Drawing in a deep breath, he nodded before stepping back, giving me space. "Good night, Imani."

"Good night, Quinn." I strode out of the kitchen, feeling the heat of his gaze on my back.

CHAPTER 17
IMANI

A shudder raced through my body just thinking about the monster in my dream—an enormous white wolf with intense brown eyes chasing me through a storm-swept forest in the dark. I was terrified and cold as I pushed through brush and branches. Tired of being hunted, I stopped to face my tormentor, the white wolf. "Why won't you stop chasing me?" I demanded.

The animal halted, staring at me silently before growling, "Not until you wake up and accept what we are." Then the wolf attacked, catching my hand in its powerful jaws, biting it off.

Kicking off my sheets, I lay there as the moonlight streamed across the bed. There was no way I'd be able to get back to sleep anytime soon. And I knew from experience that if I couldn't fall asleep, it was better to get up and do something soothing to get my mind and body in a restful state.

I walked over to the door and opened it. Peeking out, I saw it was dark and quiet. Quinn was probably sleeping. I crept down the stairs and into the kitchen. Opening the refrigerator, I pulled out a bottle of sparkling water and opened it greedily. Guzzling the contents, I moaned with pleasure as the cool, bubbly liquid rolled over my tongue.

"Couldn't sleep?" Quinn drawled.

I jumped and quickly turned around, watching as he ran a hand through his sleep-tousled hair.

Damn, no man should look this fucking good. And here I was standing in his kitchen with tangled hair, wearing an old camisole and sleep shorts.

"No. Did I wake you?" Leaning my hip against the granite kitchen counter, I boldly roamed my eyes up and down his body. The man was tanned with bulging muscles. Hardened abs rippled downward to his low-slung lounge pants.

"Not really. Your delicious scent kept fucking with my head." His gravelly voice sent lust through my body.

He came closer, making no attempt to conceal the erection tenting the lightweight fabric of his pants. My pussy clenched, imagining him filling me. Pumping hard inside. Making me come hard while my nails scraped against his back.

This man is going to be the death of me. I cleared my throat. *Get it together. Focus.*

I drained my bottle and set it down. "Guess I'll get back upstairs."

He stepped forward, caging me, making sure my body was flush against his. "I can smell your arousal," he whispered in my ear. "You want me."

I sucked in a breath as the hard bulge pressed against my stomach.

He was right. I wanted him. He growled, and the sound unclipped the leash on my restraint. Reaching between us, I gripped his thick, long cock.

He shut his eyes as a growl rumbled in his chest.

I gave him one more squeeze. His eyes opened and zeroed in on me. Our mouths were a breath away, the desire and tension almost more than I could take.

He leaned into me. "I'm trying so hard not to slam you onto this counter and ram my cock into you."

"Why don't you?" I challenged. "Maybe a good hard fuck is

what we both need." I ran my fingers across his chest. "One night."

He inhaled sharply before pulling back. "You're mine." He watched me closely, the look in his eyes making me feel beautiful and precious. "Don't you understand that I want more from you and us?"

"Quinn, what you want is not something I'm capable of giving you." I cupped his cheek. My pulse picked up a little when his eyes changed. I could feel the slide of his wolf underneath my fingers. His inner beast was so close to the surface.

"I can see and feel your wolf," I whispered, wanting him to wrap his arms around me, allowing me to curl up in his lap for the rest of the night.

"He's anxious to meet you." He brushed his hand down my back. "He wants me to claim you. Fuck you. Make you mine."

His words set my body aflame.

"Are you ready to submit to me?"

"I don't have the best track record with men. I've tried this… relationship thing, but it never works."

He plunged his tongue into my mouth, cutting off my words. He tasted like mint and sugar, and I wanted more. He tugged hard on my lip before easing back to trail scorching hot kisses across my jaw, then down to the hollow of my throat.

"More," I demanded, wrapping my arms around his neck, clinging to him.

"You're a greedy little thing." His voice was a velvet whisper against my ear. "And it's making me so hot."

I squawked when he lifted me, setting me on the countertop. He gently pushed me back, one hand firmly grabbing ahold of my wrists, while his legs forced my knees apart. His free hand tugged off my shorts.

"Good. You're not wearing panties."

I moaned with pleasure when he slid two fingers into my pussy. "Yes. More." I rode his fingers.

"Are you ready to give me what I need? What we both need?"

"What do you want, Quinn?" I wanted to come all over his fingers.

He stilled my hips. "I already told you. I want your submission. I want your body, heart, and soul. I want your beautiful body under me, over me, whatever way I can think of—for the rest of our lives."

For the rest of our lives?

Is he kidding me?

I tried to move away from him, but he held me tight.

"Quinn, I don't do relationships. I have sex."

"And shifters don't play games like humans. We know the difference between straight-up physical attraction and something more. This, between us, is something more."

"Let me up," I whispered.

He released my wrists and removed his fingers from my pussy.

"Trust me, Imani." He leaned in and kissed my throat before biting the spot. "Submit."

"I can't." It was too risky to open up my heart, only to have it broken.

"Can't? Or won't?" he asked while rubbing his nose against my neck.

"What difference does it make?" I snapped. "The answer is no."

"Is that your final answer?" he growled.

"Yes."

He sighed. "Okay." He moved away from me, offering me his hand, pulling me off the countertop. He kissed me hard on the lips before stepping back.

"See you in the morning, darling."

My heart thumped hard in my chest.

"No," I blurted out. "You won't. Staying here is a big mistake."

Muscular forearms crossed in front of him while he stared pointedly at me.

"I think it's best that I move out of your ranch," I continued. "Nyx offered me a room at her place if I want."

I steeled myself for a gaze of hatred, but his eyes remained neutral.

"I can't say that I'm not disappointed." He spoke in a quiet, rough voice.

"Quinn, I'm—"

He growled and reached over, pulling me to him as he pressed his lips to mine. He broke the kiss, giving me one last swipe of his tongue before he bit my lower lip.

"I'll be here when you're ready to stop running from us," he said before turning on his heel and exiting the kitchen.

CHAPTER 18
IMANI

Staring into the mirror while brushing my hair, I marveled at the difference a week made. I felt transformed. My senses were heightening. Even from my position in the bathroom, looking into the reflection in the mirror, I could see the flecks within the grout outlining the tiles in the shower stall. It would be only a matter of time before my inner animal would officially make its debut—letting me and everyone in the Ridge know what type of shifter I was.

I sighed deeply. Not that my shifting into my animal would make those who hated hybrids view me any differently. I'd seen the disdainful glares they gave me while I walked through Main Square.

"Imani," Nyx called from downstairs. "Are we going for our morning run or not? I have a yoga class at one."

"Hold your horses," I called while marching down the stairs.

Living with Nyx had been easier, and more fun, than I'd expected. There was no awkward breaking-in time while taking up temporary residence at her place. In fact, we quickly fell into a daily routine—breakfast together, followed by each of us going our separate ways for work. In the evenings, we'd have copious glasses of wine with our dinner after a long day at work.

Adding to my new life, my job with Piper was fabulous. She not only wanted me involved with the design of the B and B kitchen and dining area; she wanted my input on everything inside. Being a part of such an extensive project that was integral to Black Forest was exciting, but it also meant long hours at the B and B.

Reaching the bottom of the stairs, I stepped into the large parlor-dining room-music room combination with spectacular views of Main Square.

"You know New Yorkers would kill for this place," I said while striding across the pine floors and into the eat-in kitchen.

"Yup," Nyx agreed, sipping her coffee.

I poured myself a cup before taking a huge gulp.

"I lucked out getting this place," she explained. "When I moved back to the Ridge, I wanted to open a yoga studio, but nothing available felt right. Not until Old Man Daniel decided he wanted to move farther inland." She shrugged. "I didn't hesitate to purchase his historic building overlooking Main Square." She gestured around. "Now every morning, I roll out of bed and head downstairs to my yoga studio."

I grinned. "It's a damn sweet setup if you ask me and very reminiscent of the days when many shopkeepers lived above their shops."

"It's absolutely fabulous. A lot of business owners along the Main Square street have a similar setup. The Ridge is a beautiful town. You just have to look past the crazies to see it." Nyx smiled at me, tucking her cell into the pocket of her leggings. "Now let's go see the lovable crazies."

Single file, we trotted down the narrow steps that led to the street door. Once outside, I jogged in place while Nyx locked the door, then we took off in an easy run.

"End of the block, make a left," Nyx instructed.

Doing as told, we ended up by a lake with clear, glistening waters. With both of us jogging in place, she explained, "This is one of the Ridge's most scenic spots. It's called Bogbeast Lake."

Due to long hours at work, I hadn't taken the time to sight-see, so I enjoyed getting this tour. "It's stunning," I whispered. The waters were crystal clear and extended for miles. I blinked when I caught a group of big splashes farther out. "What's that?" I pointed to the area.

"Could be mermen-shifters or a selkie," she answered and then took off in a jog. "Let's go. We have more to see."

I sped up, easily keeping pace beside her. "Mermen or selkie?" I squeaked. "Are you fucking with me? I thought mermaids were folklore." I knew about the legends of the half-fish/half-human creatures called mermaids, but I had never heard of a selkie.

"There are no mermaids in the lake, just mermen. And it's not a legend, it's real."

Mermen are real?

"So what is a selkie?" I asked.

"Selkies are seal-shifters. While in the sea, their bottom halves have a seal's tail, but their upper halves remain human."

My eyes widened. "Wow. Next you'll tell me that the kraken is real."

"It is."

I stumbled, then righted myself.

"What?" She briefly glanced at me. "There are many unique and nearly extinct species of Others that live in the Ridge. That's what makes this town so special. It's also what makes most of the residents so paranoid about strangers. They've suffered so much at the hands of humans."

Mulling over her words, I replied, "I have no intention of harming them."

"I know that. I'm just giving you some insight that will help you understand that, for most of them, it's not hatred that fuels them—it's fear."

With a couple of sweeps around the perimeter, we made it back to the heart of Main Square. Across the street, a huge black

SUV pulled up in front of a place called Bessie's Coffee Shop, and a familiar man hopped out.

"Oh, look. There's Mack," Nyx said. "Hey, Mack," she called out with a wave but continued to run past him.

I also gave him a wave and a "Hi!"

He tipped his hat, continuing inside Bessie's.

"Is that a popular place?" I asked.

"Best coffee in town. And I'm not just saying that because she's my coven sister."

When we approached Quinn's forge and Emmett's garage, I eyed Quinn's vehicle parked outside.

Nyx jogged to a stop. "You want to go in and say hi to your wolf?" She winked at me.

"He's not my wolf." I stretched my arms to loosen my muscles.

"Sure he's not." Nyx grinned.

I gave her the stink eye. "Things between Quinn and me are a little weird right now."

"Why?" She placed her hands on her hips.

I wanted to say because I hadn't seen or spoken to him in days, but instead, I said, "When I told him I'd be staying with you, he wasn't pleased."

"Aha," Nyx said. "Now I understand what's going on between you two." She glanced around. "Let's take a break and walk a bit."

Main Square was getting more crowded, so I didn't mind the respite.

"Imani, Quinn wasn't happy about you staying with me because you're his fated mate. He wanted you to be with him."

"I need space. I'm not going to rush into a relationship with him because of his blind belief that we're destined to be together."

"Blind belief?" Nyx replied. "Is that what you think fated mates are?"

"I know sex. I don't understand romantic relationships or love." *Or trust*, I left unsaid.

"Interesting." Nyx gave me the side-eye.

"Interesting? What does that mean?"

She waved to someone across the street. "I've seen that expression on your face before. You're terrified of falling in love with him."

"Maybe." I increased my pace. "I mean, what if this fated-mate thing doesn't work out between us?"

"What if it does?" She skidded to a stop.

I blew past her and then doubled back. "The whole concept of fated mates freaks me the hell out."

She tilted her head, examining me. "Why?"

"Because I don't believe in soul mates or being with any man forever."

"You mean, you don't believe in love."

"No, I don't," I admitted. "Love is utter bullshit. People throw that word around like confetti. But in the end, when things get rough, all that love stuff goes right out the window, and they walk away." Like my biological mother did to me.

"So you're scared shitless of letting him into your heart." It was a statement, not a question.

I narrowed my eyes on her. "Yes." And that was my truth.

"That's what I thought." She started walking again, this time slowly. "Growing up in this town, I hated everything about it. That everyone is always up in my business. That I'd never be able to step out from my mom's shadow." She glanced at me. "Then one summer, I met this guy. He came to the Ridge to spend time with his grandfather, Shane. It was love at first sight—for me, not for him. Long story short, I did some pretty nasty shit to the residents in this town, all in the name of love. He dumped me after I woke up to the reality of his bullshit lies and manipulation. I was so ashamed of all the fucked-up things I'd done to my mom and the townsfolk that I left the Ridge to try to find myself again."

My eyes widened. "And did you?"

"I did." She smiled. "I also discovered that honest people still exist in this world. You just have to break through your fear to find them."

"It's not that easy," I protested.

"Never said it was. But hiding behind an emotional wall because you're afraid to let people in isn't easy either. Believe me, I know."

Nyx stopped in front of a storefront with an Izzy's Herbal Apothecary & Supply sign and a hand-painted window that promised Herbs, Oils, Teas, Tinctures. "Let's go inside. Izzy is dying to meet you."

We walked inside a large, light-filled room that made it easy to see the wide array of remedies on offer at the apothecary. The shop had a smattering of customers who nodded and said hello to Nyx and me, then continued their shopping.

I returned everyone's greeting. "Well, at least they're friend-ly," I said.

"You see." Nyx nudged me. "Not every person in town is a total asshat."

Nyx waved at the woman with high cheekbones and a blond buzz cut who was standing behind a counter in front of a wall of dried herbs. "Hi, Nyx. Hi, Imani. Welcome. I'll be with you in a minute after I ring up these customers."

"Hi," we both said in unison.

Nyx walked over to talk to someone on the other side of the store.

I strolled over to a wall of alphabetized herbs and tiny, cool little implements and containers. "This store is genius," I mumbled under my breath, peeping at the teeny tiny herbal scoops that were like Monopoly pieces but more functional. Fascinated, I went over to an octagonal, antique-looking spin-ning display in the back right corner.

I didn't even notice that Izzy was by my side until she said, "I salvaged that display from an old hardware store in town."

"I love it. It's a testament to craftsmanship that doesn't exist anymore," I replied.

"Sure doesn't." She smiled. "Welcome to the Ridge, Imani. I'm sorry I couldn't make it to the town hall meeting. Heidi, the sheriff's administrative assistant, who's also a bunny-shifter, went into labor, and I had to be there for her delivery."

"You're a midwife?"

"Nope. I'm the town healer. I was there in case her delivery didn't go well. But this town will sure need a midwife if fated mates start coming to the Ridge. Well, that's the hope." She grinned, looping her arm through mine. "I make everything in here from scratch." She pointed at the welcoming space, stocked top to bottom with tinctures and teas, soaps and lotions, and endless herbal blends.

"Really?"

"Yes, and it's all laced with my special brand of magic." She wiggled her fingers.

She guided me to the front. "I also make oil rollers that dispense tinctures to treat everything from headaches to crow's-feet."

"Izzy, you had me at oil."

A half hour later, I'd purchased several items that Izzy promised to have delivered to Nyx's place.

Nyx tugged me away from the counter. "Time to go." She glanced over at Izzy. "We're partying at the saloon Friday night. Are you coming?"

"Hell no!" Izzy answered. "Every time I party with you, I wake up the next morning with Mr. Wrong in my bed."

"Yet you still show up when we have girls' night," Nyx said.

Izzy sighed dramatically. "The devil makes me do it."

"Sure he does." Nyx grinned.

I called out, "See you Friday, Izzy," as Nyx dragged me out the door.

"Maybe," Izzy returned with a wink.

CHAPTER 19
IMANI

"Come on, Imani," Nyx crooned, tugging me into a posh-looking Rebellious Rose boutique that would fit right in on Madison Avenue.

"Why do I have to buy an outfit?" I demanded. "I already have a good pair of jeans to wear for drinks."

My eyes scanned the store, and frankly, everything I saw looked out of my budget. Eclectic music floated through the air, matching the relaxed but upscale ambiance of the boutique. The space was small but sleek and very glam. The walls were painted black, which allowed the rich, vibrant colors of the clothing on display to pop against the beautiful darkness.

Nyx shoved me forward gently. "Because we're going out for drinks, not for coffee at Bessie's."

Two customers gave me the stink eye, moving away from me like I had the plague.

One woman hissed, "We don't want you in our town, hybrid."

I turned to face her head-on. "Well, that's unfortunate," I said coolly. "For you. Because I'm staying."

"Was that clear enough for you, Ingrid?" Nyx pointed in Ingrid's face. "Now go run tell that to your surfeit."

Without another word, Ingrid stormed out.

"Nyx, what the hell is a surfeit?"

"A group of skunks. Ingrid's a skunk-shifter."

I arched a brow. "And how big do these skunks get when they shift?"

"Typically, the size of a house cat." Nyx used her hands to approximate the size.

"Well, that's scary." I shivered at the concept of Others shifting into skunks.

"Anyhow," Nyx said, dragging me farther into the boutique, "forget about Ingrid. She doesn't speak for everyone in this town."

I knew she didn't, but her outburst still bothered me.

Distracted by my thoughts, I started when I heard a husky voice say, "Nyx, my favorite person." A lanky woman dressed in all red leather sped over, wrapping her arms around Nyx.

Nyx hugged her and then stepped back. "Imani, this is Rose, my friend. She's a doe—a female deer-shifter."

I admired Rose's pouf of reddish-brown hair with pristine white streaks.

"Nice to meet you, Rose." I leaned forward to shake her hand; Rose pulled me into a big hug.

"I don't shake hands," Rose admonished. "I'm a hugger." She pulled away, giving me an impish smile. "Welcome to my little piece of glam paradise."

"Thank you," I replied. "Your boutique is lovely."

She smiled. "Thank you. Everything in here I designed and made with my nimble little fingers." She looped her arm through mine, escorting me over to side-by-side racks of beautiful clothing.

She released me, pulling out a leather corset and skirt, handing both to me. "This is my latest creation." She looked me over with a gleam of appreciation. "Your body is a perfect foil for my clothes."

"Your pieces are beautiful," I whispered. The design, cut, and stitching were impeccable, and it didn't help that I had a secret addiction to high-end leather goods.

"I love it," Nyx squealed. "Imani, try it on."

Looking at the price tag, I frowned. "I really shouldn't." I was on a budget and couldn't afford to splurge on nonessential stuff.

"Please," Rose pleaded. "Try it on. I don't get enough customers in this town who appreciate leather as you obviously do." She took the pieces from me. "Let me set you up in a fitting room." She and Nyx didn't give me a choice. They nudged me into the room with the items.

I sighed heavily, stripping and donning the leather clothing. "Sweet baby Jesus," I whispered, checking myself out in the mirror. Everything about me in this outfit was a smoking ten.

"Get out here," Nyx demanded. "I want to see it."

Opening the door, I strutted out. "What do you think?" I turned left and right like I was posing on a fashion show runway.

"Hot!" Nyx cried. "Get it now."

I shook my head. "I can't. Did you see the price tag? It's too—"

"Expensive for the likes of you," a cold female voice interjected.

"Excuse me?" I spun around to stare at the person who'd made that offensive statement. It was the redhead Quinn had snubbed a couple of mornings ago and who had also been at the Sam mob.

"Skedaddle, Prudence," Nyx said.

Prudence shrugged. "I'm just stating the facts." She walked over, standing within inches of me, using her height as intimidation. Up close, I had to admit the woman was beautiful. Her hair was a mass of red perfection, and her porcelain skin was flawless. But that was only outer beauty. I could tell by the haughty look in her blue eyes and the way her lip curled upward into an icy smile that Prudence was evil on the inside.

Rose sped over so fast that she was a blur. "Prudence, if you can't keep it classy, then get the hell out of my shop."

"You actually think you snared Quinn?" Prudence directed to me.

I definitely disliked her.

"What?" I asked. *Is this chick serious?* "Quinn and I are not dating." My body appeared languid, but inside, I was prepared for anything from this viper.

Prudence tossed her hair over her shoulder. "Don't give me that shit. Everyone knows you were staying at his ranch, spreading your legs for him."

I fought to tamp down my anger. I'd dealt with mean girls like Prudence all my life, and I knew from experience that the best way to get under their skin was to kill them with my cool and collected verbal shanking. "So what you're saying is you're scared that my pussy is better than yours?"

Prudence stiffened. "You're nothing compared to a full-blood wolf-shifter like me. He'll never make you alpha female of this town."

I arched a brow. "Are you sure about that?"

A tic started below Prudence's eye, a sign I'd gotten under her skin. *Gotcha, skank.*

"That's a given," Prudence responded. "Quinn is mine."

"Prudence!" Nyx and Rose yelled in unison.

"I got this, y'all," I said to both women.

Nyx stuck up her middle finger at Prudence.

Prudence smiled. "He hasn't mated for a reason."

I contemplated telling her that I was his fated mate, but I decided against it. I wasn't going to accept Quinn's claim.

"Probably because he's smart enough not to confuse a sloppy one-night stand with a woman he'd actually mate," I suggested.

"How dare you!" she sputtered. "He'll never mate a hybrid, and I will not stand by while you try to steal him away from me."

Damn, this woman is batshit crazy.

"Watch me." I batted my eyes dramatically. "Look, I'm done playing around with you. So here's what you're going to do. You're going to take your skinny ass out of this shop and leave me alone. End of story."

Prudence stepped closer. "How about I shift and fucking tear your ass into so many pieces Quinn won't even recognize you?"

The patrons in the store inched closer but pretended not to be listening to our argument.

That's it. I've had enough.

Bickering was one thing, but threatening to kill me?

Prudence had crossed the damn line of no return.

"What did you say?" My voice was barely audible.

Her eyes were icy. "I said I will rip you to shreds. Am I clear enough, hybrid?"

I clenched my hands. "The only thing that's keeping me from beating the living shit out of you is that I don't want blood getting all over Rose's beautiful clothing. I'm giving you five seconds to walk away before I change my damn mind and show you exactly what a hybrid can do."

Prudence took a step back. "This is not the end of this," she promised before stomping away like I'd stolen her fucking bike and exiting the store.

"Good riddance," Rose chirped.

I stared at both of them. "What is her deal?"

"A one-night stand gone horribly wrong," Nyx answered. "The entire town knows about it."

I shook my head. "Apparently nothing is private in Black Forest."

"Nope," Nyx said. "Prudence has been chasing Quinn since they were teens. And she hasn't caught him yet because he's not interested in her."

"Well, he dipped his cock in that whirlwind of crazy, so he must have stopped running," I asserted.

"Once, five years ago, and he's been regretting that shit every day," Nyx said.

Nyx's words confirmed that Prudence was the woman Quinn had told me he'd slept with.

Rose clucked her tongue. "We've grown up with Prudence, and believe me, she's been a psycho wolf-shifter all her life."

"So she was part of his pack?" I asked.

"Not anymore," Nyx replied. "She belongs to the Jenkins pack, one town over. Her father used to be the beta for Quinn's father. Then he got kicked out of the Bane pack when some shady shit went down with her father and some unmated females."

Rose chimed in, "Prudence and her father left the Ridge in shame, but it hasn't stopped her from stalking Quinn every day."

"But never mind her," Nyx announced. "Let's get back to you." She walked around me, eyeing my outfit. "Perfection. Buy it."

I shook my head. "It's gorgeous, but I can't afford it. I simply don't have the cash."

"Cash?" Rose arched a brow. "You don't need no stinking cash. Most of us barter around here. Now how I hear it, you've got mad cooking skills."

"You heard right," I boasted, giving her a sassy grin.

"Great. Because the deer-mating matchup is approaching, and I need you to teach me how to make delicious man-catching vegetarian dishes. How about one cooking lesson, and I'll give you that outfit for free?"

"Rose, I can't allow you to undervalue your beautiful work," I said. This scrumptious buttery leather goodness was a high three digits. "Three cooking lessons and we have a deal."

Rose pulled me into a hug and squealed, "Deal."

CHAPTER 20
IMANI

After a quick shower and grabbing something to eat, I headed out of Nyx's building and over to Piper's B and B to start my day at work. It was a short walk, and the weather was perfect for my stroll. As I walked down the sidewalk, a couple of townsfolk milling around Main Square waved with welcoming smiles, and I returned their greeting. I passed many more residents, and they purposely insulted me by ignoring me.

I snorted at their deliberate snub. I'd learned from my time in the foster care system that the best way to deal with ignorance was to not overreact and that maybe, in time, their grudges would fly away—if not, fuck them.

I smiled at the people I saw wearing white buttons with the slogan I LOVE HYBRIDS. Piper and Freya had had the buttons made, passing them out to townsfolk to wear as a show of solidarity.

Finally reaching the corner-lot B and B that faced Main Square, I stopped by the hot spring water fountain in front of the B and B, filling my water bottle. Afterward, I took a sip while standing outside on the sidewalk, just staring at the absolutely stunning historical gem of beauty and elegance. Piper had told me it had been built in 1924 and that it had sat unoccupied for years until she turned it into a B and B.

Opening the iron fence, I strode past the gardens, sauntered up the front stairs, and pushed open the unlocked door that gave access to the workers hired to renovate the house. When I stepped inside, I heard none of the loud noise of construction, which meant Jasper's workers hadn't arrived yet.

I took the silence as an opportunity to see the work done, walking around the large rooms that were flooded with natural daylight.

"This is beautiful."

The architectural details were endless, from Italian marble mantels, crystal chandeliers, crown moldings, massive windows, to spectacular wood floors.

"Imani," Piper called out.

"I'm in the grand ballroom," I answered.

I heard the clicking of her heels against the wood floors before she entered the room.

"I love this place, Piper." I gestured to the two tall carved-manteled fireplaces and the crystal chandelier.

"I do too, but it's going to take a lot of work to restore it to its original splendor." She smiled at me. "And once we get the kitchen done to your specifications, then we'll have your wonderful food to serve the guests. Come. Let's look upstairs. I want to get your feedback on what they've finished."

We walked upstairs side by side.

"Are you going to expand the number of bedrooms?" I asked.

"No. I think seven bedrooms, each with baths and fireplaces, are enough. And with the sun-room spanning the entire rear of the home, I think the guests will enjoy the layout."

We entered each room one by one.

"What if the mating spell brings more women than expect-ed?" I persisted.

"I hope the call brings lots of fated mates, but my B and B is only a temporary place for them to stay until they find their mate." She paused. "I heard you made the rounds in town today with Nyx. Everyone has pleasant things to say about you."

I shrugged. "Mostly, the people are friendly. I like that."

We made our way back down to the main level and into the bright area that would soon be the dining room and kitchen with breakfast area.

"Townsfolk are not all like Sam," Piper said.

"Or like Prudence?" I added.

She stopped to stare at me. "No. And thank goodness for that."

I strode over to the French doors facing the rear grounds and stared at the blooming magnolias.

Piper walked up to my left. "Quinn misses your presence at the ranch."

Turning to face her, I said, "Did he also tell you that I'm not going to accept his mating claim?"

"Why?"

There was no sense beating around the bush. She deserved to hear the truth.

"I've been left, hurt, disappointed, and let down in the past," I said simply. "There's no way I'd risk going through that pain again."

"Quinn would never hurt you."

In my heart, I knew that being vulnerable was a risky choice I wasn't sure I wanted to take.

"Not intentionally." I sighed heavily. "Do you really think that our relationship can stand the wrath of the town once they find out I'm his fated mate?"

"Yes, I do. But change is not easy. It takes work and perseverance."

"Piper…"

"Imani." She grabbed my arms. "I'm not asking you to plan

your future right now. All I'm saying is just live in the here and now. Tomorrow is not promised to anyone, but today, that's where all the magic happens."

"One day at a time," I answered. "That's all I can promise."

"I'll take it."

CHAPTER 21
IMANI

Staring at myself in the mirror, I looked quite good.

My zipper-front leather bustier corset top exposed the expanse of my dark skin while hugging my hourglass curves.

My long legs sported a short leather skirt paired with leather ankle wedge boots with a rubber outsole for stability.

"You look great," Nyx said from her perch at the edge of my bed.

I turned to the side with my hands on my waist. "But if I bend over, you'll see my ass cheeks."

Nyx winked. "Isn't that the point?"

"No. It isn't." I chuckled. "We're going out for drinks. Not to pick up shifters."

"Speak for yourself," Nyx countered.

"Harlot," I retorted with a smirk.

My cell pinged. Grabbing it, I swiped the screen. "It's a text from Emmett. He's finished with my car." I glanced over at Nyx. "While you're getting ready, I'll walk over to his shop and pay him. Swing by and get me when you're done, then we'll head over to the saloon."

"Sounds like a plan." Nyx stood up and stretched. "And say hi to Quinn for me."

My heart thudded at the mere mention of his name. Just the thought of seeing him filled me with happiness and trepidation. "It's late. What makes you think I'll see him?"

"Because according to Piper, he's been spending a hell of a lot of time at his forge"—she made air quotes—"'working' since you've been staying with me. He misses you, as you do him." She winked and then sauntered away.

When I entered Emmett's garage, no one was there, so I tested the door to the forge. It was open.

I walked inside what looked like converted stables. The space was enormous, with a stone forge that took up the entire back wall. Several racks of forged iron artwork lined the walls, along with bins of raw materials and shelves of tools.

"Hey," Quinn said, standing up from his workbench.

Jesus, he was the most beautiful man I'd ever laid eyes on. Dressed in jeans and a plaid button-up shirt, he should have appeared nonthreatening, but I could see the wildness in his eyes.

"Hey," I replied, watching him warily.

I barely resisted the strange urge to run to him and throw myself into his arms. But I refused to give in to my need for him. No matter how much I'd missed him.

"You look awful fancy." His eyes roamed over me from head to toe, making my skin tingle as though he'd actually stroked me. "Where you heading tonight?" His lips curved, making me long to press my own against his.

"Out for drinks with Nyx," I replied a little breathlessly. "I was looking for Emmett. He said my car is ready, so I wanted to pay him."

He wiped his hands on a black cloth. "He's over at Bessie's, grabbing pie. He'll be back in a few." His gaze raked over me, heating every inch of my skin in its path.

His mouth curved, and I realized I'd been staring at his lips. The knowledge that he knew exactly what he did to me glittered in his eyes. Startled by my reaction, I struggled to gather my thoughts.

"I should go now," I croaked, my palms suddenly sweaty.

"Why?" His nostrils flared. "He'll be back in a few." He hadn't moved from his position by the workbench.

Imani, stop acting like a startled animal ready to bolt.

This is Quinn.

He won't bite you…

Drawing in a deep breath, I spun around, taking in all the artwork that was either nature-themed, of animals, or mythological creatures. In the center of the room was a large, sinuous dragon, clearly a sculpture in midconstruction.

"The artwork is amazing," I commented, staring at the mesmerizing masterpieces.

"Thank you. I do a lot of large commission pieces, but sometimes the pack and I work on projects together. I smith full time. My dad taught me, and when I came back home, I decided to open this shop."

I cast a quick glance at him only to find him watching me.

He walked over to the dragon and patted its side, where the oval scales with an iridescent patina were being welded on. "This is a commission for a man in New Orleans. Our sculptures have gotten popular, and now I can sell them and make some extra money for the town." He looked up at the dragon, which towered over him by several feet. "This baby's going to be installed in a park, and it will buy folks here a new wing on the library."

He cooks and bakes.

And he's a philanthropist?

This has to be some kind of joke.

He seems too good to be true.

Turning around, I stared at him. "It's really outstanding work, Quinn. I like it, a lot."

He strode toward me like an animal stalking its prey. He grabbed my hand, and heat raced up my arm. I gasped and attempted to pull away, but he closed his other hand over mine, holding my trembling one cupped between them.

Struggling to breathe normally, I felt my heart nearly pound out of my chest.

"Imani?"

"Yes?" I stopped fighting his firm but gentle grip.

"You can't run from destiny," he said softly. His large hands holding mine felt scorching hot as he stared at me hungrily, making the casual gesture far too intimate.

He continued, "You're mine."

My fingers trembled.

He tilted his head and studied me. "Imani, trust me to love, cherish, and protect you."

Oh God. He's melting my heart.

Making me want more than I'm capable of giving.

To love and be loved.

I snatched my hands away. "Quinn, there is so much you don't know about me. So much we don't know about each other."

"Give us time."

Fear twisted in my stomach.

He cupped my cheek. "Let me into your heart."

Despite my best efforts, hearing the emotions lacing his words cracked the shell protecting my heart.

"Quinn, it's been days since I left your ranch. You didn't call me. You didn't try."

"I was giving you space. I didn't want to pressure you into giving me something that you're not ready to give. Trust and love. But you are here, and deep down inside, you know there is something between us worth fighting for. You're just too scared to acknowledge it."

The truth of his words told me he saw me.

The real me that had shut down my heart so it could not be hurt again.

"I'm broken," I croaked. "And you deserve more." *There. I said it. My truth.* I was broken in too many ways to count.

"Imani, your past doesn't define you."

I arched a brow. "Doesn't it? I've never been important to anyone."

He kissed my forehead. "You're important to me."

"Quinn, I'm still so haunted by the memories of all the people in my dysfunctional past who were incapable of loving me unconditionally. They all gave up on me at the first sight of my imperfection, and given time, you will too."

"Imani, if you really believe that, then you haven't learned shit about me. And just so we're clear, I'm not giving up on you."

"Quinn, magic brought me here. This is not real or true."

"This is real." He settled his warm hands on my shoulders. The heat from his hands spread, warming me all over. The rush of pleasure raced through me.

"But how can we ever know?" I whispered.

A plethora of warnings against continuing down this path with him swirled in my head.

What if the town turns on me again?

Will he fight to keep me? Or just like everyone else in my past, will he betray me and throw me out like trash?

"The heart doesn't lie." He spoke in a rough voice. "You just have to trust enough to listen to it." His voice whispered against my ear, "Do you want us?"

Despite the fear slithering through my veins, I wanted him. I wanted to try for something real. I'd never met a man I wanted to risk it all with—until Quinn.

I nodded while my heart thumped hard in my chest.

"Words, Imani. Tell me what you want."

"I want us. But you need to understand that it won't be easy. Our relationship will take work."

"I wouldn't have it any other way." Then he dipped his head and planted those gorgeous lips of his on mine.

Wrapping my arms around his waist, I sighed deeply when he cradled my body in his arms.

He lightly caressed the exposed skin between the waist of my skirt and the edge of my corset. I could feel my nipples poking against the leather of my bustier, and I was aware that my panties were getting wet. I rocked against him, reveling in the hardness that pushed into my belly.

My breasts pressed to his hard chest, his muscular legs against mine.

He touched a sensitive spot on my neck with his lips, one I hadn't even known I had. Quinn darted his tongue out and caressed it intimately before giving me a small nip that sent jolts of fire racing through my nerve endings.

He moved his tongue to trace along my chin as he skimmed my stomach with his hands.

Everything outside of Quinn was a stream of incoherent sounds. There was something different about him and my primal reaction to him.

Groaning, I moved my hand up and through his mass of thick hair as we kissed. He broke our kiss, his eyes dilated and breathing heavy. He pulled down the zipper on the front of my bustier corset top, exposing my skin to the cool air. When he caressed my nipples, I moaned.

He dropped to his knees before me to suck at my pebbled peaks. "You taste delicious," he groaned.

"And your tongue feels like heaven," I said.

I'd never been a foreplay kind of chick, but the feel of Quinn's tongue against my skin made me realize what I'd been missing. I barely felt it when he unzipped my skirt, pushing down my panties. Both items pooled by my ankles. He used his fingers to play with the short, trimmed hairs of my pussy.

There was something kinky and thrilling about being

exposed to Quinn out in the open in the forge, where anyone could see us.

Getting to his feet, he lifted me, and instinctively, I wrapped my legs around his waist, allowing him to carry me over to a workbench, where he seated me on top. Dropping to his knees, he wedged himself between my legs, his hand cupping my sex, and I began gyrating against him in wild excitement.

I shuddered and cried out when his thick finger parted my folds and flicked over the hardened bud at my cunt.

"Fuck!" I moaned as his magic fingers worked me hard.

He pressed and circled, all the while kissing, sucking, and licking at pleasure points I'd never discovered with any other man but him. I felt the familiar clenching in the pit of my belly and the searing-hot pressure of an orgasm exploding and washing over me.

CHAPTER 22
QUINN

Sensing Imani's cresting orgasm, I pressed my finger into her body. She threw back her head, exposing the long and graceful curve of her neck. I withdrew my finger and gently worked it back in. She moaned with pleasure. My cock hardened further. I worked my finger slowly, pushing it forward, then retreating in response to her body's reaction.

"Quinn," Imani cried out.

I growled, sensing the emotions running through her as if they were in my body. It was a connection I'd never experienced before.

Mine, my inner beast declared. I wanted her just as badly as my animal did, but not here in the forge.

Imani's hands tightened, almost painfully, in my hair. I nuzzled her thigh, quickening the movements of my finger as it stroked her.

Frantic cries erupted from her throat, and her pussy clenched down as she came apart. Watching her face, I memorized the small lines that appeared on her forehead as she came.

I struggled to regain control. My eyes closed. After some seconds, her hands landed on my shoulders, and just like that, my eyes opened and I'd regained my control, tugging her against me.

"What's wrong?" she whispered.

"The first time I take you, I want you in my bed, where I can worship your body like the goddess you are. I want to kiss you here…" I slid my hand against her calf.

Pushing off my knees, I stood, then lifted her off the workbench to stand. "And here…" I let my hands trail up the backs of her thighs until they came to land against her ass. I pulled her forward, and she whimpered.

"Imani?" Nyx yelled from outside.

Imani swallowed hard.

I growled at the interruption.

"Quinn?" Nyx called.

I remained silent. Imani pressed her forehead against my chest.

"I know you're here, Quinn," Nyx bellowed, "Your truck is out front."

Imani started chuckling.

"Whatever you two are doing," Nyx started, "quit it. I'm taking her out for drinks at the Cauldron. I'll be outside in my car, Imani."

Then there was silence.

Imani walked over to her clothes and dressed.

"She's a pain in the ass," I mumbled.

"Yup, but I like her. So be nice." Imani smirked as she came toward me.

"To be continued?" I asked.

"It's a date." She touched my cheek before turning on her heels, sauntering away with a seductive sway to her hips.

An hour later, sitting at my workbench, I stared into space, amazed that in days Imani had changed my world as I knew it.

She was mine, and I looked forward to a lifetime with her by my side.

My cell rang. "Any trouble?" I answered.

For Imani's safety, unbeknownst to her, Jasper and Brody had been trailing Imani and Nyx for days. Even though the town hall meeting was a success, a lot of residents were still displeased about the vote in Imani's favor. Then there was Sam. I knew that crazy fucker would never rest until he killed Imani.

"Prudence," Jasper rushed out. "Brody and I saw her entering the Cauldron. Brody went inside to see if he could find her while I stayed behind to keep an eye on Imani."

"Fuck!" I scratched my chin. "And the trouble keeps coming." According to town gossip, Sam had been stirring up more chaos by whispering nasty innuendos about Imani and me in Prudence's ear. And knowing how possessive and crazy Prudence was about me, that spelled disaster.

"I'll be there in a few minutes," I barked, racing out of the forge.

CHAPTER 23
IMANI

Since I was in my thoughts, Nyx's car was silent all the way to the Cauldron Saloon. When she pulled up to the club and parked, she eyed me.

"So how was the sex with Quinn?"

"What are you talking about?" There was no way she could know what had happened between Quinn and me; she'd never come inside the forge.

"I read and sense auras, and I felt the scorching sexual energy you and Quinn were giving off as soon as I cracked open the door to the forge."

"We're working on the logistics of us. So don't start planning our wedding."

"I won't, but there's no way you're getting away with not having a mating ceremony. It's tradition." She wagged her finger at me.

I unbuckled my seat belt. "What in the hell is a mating ceremony again?"

"A formal ceremony attended by the entire town." She pulled out her car key, dropping it into her clutch purse.

I frowned. "That sounds like a wedding."

"But there's one difference. You and the alpha copulating in the forest like rabbits under the full moon." She grinned.

"I'm not interested in having outdoor sex."

"Yet. Give it time."

I shook my head. "You sound like a lunatic." I couldn't help the curl of my lips into a smile. I liked Nyx, and it was nice and different to have a real friend to hang out and talk with.

"Hey, don't shoot the messenger." She shrugged. "I'm just dropping glitter truth bombs on my new bestie." She gave me a wide grin.

"Just so you know, I hate glitter."

"Oh hell." She clutched her imaginary pearls. "Say it ain't so. Everyone loves glitter."

"I don't." I pointed to the driver's-side door with a smirk. "Now go on, get."

We stepped into the saloon, and I couldn't believe what I was seeing.

"What in the world is going on?" I asked.

The dance floor was packed with barely dressed couples gyrating and reenacting scenes from a porn movie.

Nyx smiled. "This is how the Ridge gets freaky naughty when the sun goes down. Once a month, Mom has this anything goes gathering, inviting Others from the neighboring towns to mingle."

"I think there's a lot more than mingling going on tonight." My eyes were on a woman wearing a short leather dress with her ass cheeks hanging out and thigh-high stiletto boots.

Nyx shrugged. "There's a high probability of catching partiers fucking and sucking."

I glared at her. "Don't you think you should have mentioned that when you invited me out for drinks?"

"There's no pressure to take part. I don't. But I love a good sex exhibition show."

I stared at her like she'd lost her mind. "I'm not a prude, but I'm not into voyeurism."

Nyx fluffed up her hair. "Imani, you're part of this town now, and that means you have to get to know these crazy fuckers."

She had a point. "Fine. One drink, then I'm out."

"Two drinks followed up by a round of dirty dancing in the middle of the dance floor," Nyx countered.

"Deal. You had me at dirty dancing."

Nyx grabbed my hand. "Come on, let's get some drinks—all on me." We moved through the crowd in the bar's direction, skirting along the edge of the dance floor. I tried my best to avoid a collision with the seminude, gyrating bodies. I could see flashes of Others in booths, tucked in the corner doing God knows what. Men sizing up women like cattle.

"This is a freaking sex circus," I mumbled under my breath.

"It's the best show on earth," Nyx declared.

When we finally reached the bar, Freya was working behind it alongside a lanky bartender with floppy curls and a disarming smile.

"Hi, ladies," Freya greeted.

"Hi, Freya," I returned, settling down on the leather barstool.

"It's crowded tonight, Mom," Nyx remarked while sinking down onto her own stool.

"Most of them are here to gossip about our new resident in town, Imani," Freya explained.

Nyx nudged me. "Damn, girl, you're popular."

"For all the wrong reasons," I mumbled.

Freya swayed to the beat of the music. "Who cares? I say give those judgmental fuckers something to talk about."

"Agreed," Nyx said and gave Freya a high five.

I smirked. "You witches are crazy." I grabbed a peanut from the bowl on the bar and shucked it, popping it into my mouth.

"Certifiable," Freya quipped.

Nyx followed up with, "Welcome to your new family, Imani."

I rolled my eyes, but deep inside, it warmed me how they'd both accepted me into their fold.

Freya waved at someone at the end of the bar. "Hot damn, I've just spotted man candy that's looking for company." She looked at the male bartender. "Liam, take care of my ladies." Then she drifted off without saying goodbye.

Nyx yelled after her, "Remember, no glove, no love!"

Liam beamed at us. "Ladies, how may I serve you?"

"One shot of vodka," I responded.

"The same," Nyx said.

He roamed away, and he returned minutes later with two small silver cups, placing them before us. We toasted before smelling the vodka while swirling it in our glass.

Taking a small sip, I let the flavor rest on my palate for a few seconds before swallowing it, savoring the aftertaste.

"Now let's take our asses to the dance floor," Nyx demanded. "We need to show these rhythm-challenged fuckers how it's done."

She dragged me into the crush of Others on the dance floor. I couldn't help watching how the couples were sensually touching each other. The primal way their bodies rubbed together called to something deep inside me. Heat raced through my body, making me feel like live wires were sparking under my skin.

Closing my eyes, I swayed to the beat of the music. A vision of Quinn and me together blossomed in my mind.

Him above me, taking me hard and fast as I arched and cried out under him.

Me above him, neck thrown back, as he sank his long incisors into my shoulder.

My breathing hitched.

My vision was so vivid. So real.

My eyes snapped open when I felt a pair of arms wrap around my waist. "What the...?" I hissed before being spun around to find Quinn's eyes staring down at me.

He leaned down with his lips brushing against my ear. "You're beautiful."

CHAPTER 24
QUINN

My body boiled with fury when I stepped into the Cauldron. I walked up to Jasper, who was standing in the shadows at the edge of the dance floor. "Did you find Prudence?"

He shook his head. "No. Brody is still searching."

"I'm done with this Prudence shit," I barked. "We need to find her. You take the left. I'll take the right." I started to move when the most intoxicating scent hit me.

My unease increased tenfold.

Something strange was happening.

The scent continued to grow until I could no longer think or speak. My beast tried to fight its way out. I froze and closed my eyes, willing my wolf to be at peace. But still, he battled. Man and beast warred for dominance as I located the floral scent of Imani entwined with a subtle moss and earthy aroma.

My gaze locked on Imani gyrating on the dance floor. Her scent differed from an hour ago. It had changed, heightened, and it was surrounding me in seductive waves. I couldn't turn away even if I wanted to, and I didn't.

I inhaled again, a long draw that pulled her scent into me.

Imani's inner animal was awakening, and she might not even know it.

My heart raced with excitement, because like a kid in a candy shop, I wanted to unwrap her to find out what type of shifter she was. That was when I noticed I wasn't the only unmated male intrigued by her intoxicating scent.

Mine. Fight, my beast demanded.

I lowered my head, willing him away.

My beast was in territorial mode, and if he got out, he'd rip all the unmated males to pieces.

I moved toward her, coming to a stop behind her, wrapping my arms around her waist, imagining how her sexy naked body would look riding me hard and fast.

When she turned around to face me, I growled, "You're beautiful."

She stepped closer. Her lids drooped slightly as she stared at me. Her eyes had morphed to amber right before me.

My eyes moved away from her face, traveling down her body. I could smell the luscious, tantalizing aroma of her heated sex.

She wanted me, and both man and beast preened under her unmistakable desire.

I growled softly when her pink tongue snaked out to wet her full lips. I encircled her waist with my hand, pulling her against me, letting her feel my hard arousal.

CHAPTER 25
IMANI

I blinked, not believing what I was seeing. His eyes transformed. "Quinn? Uh, your eyes. They're amber."

"As are yours. More proof that you're mine and I'm yours." He lowered his lips to mine. His kiss was soft and hard, dominant and unyielding.

I locked my hands around his neck as I undulated against him, dragging a feral-sounding groan from deep within him.

Waves of heat pulsed through my body. Sweat trickled between my breasts. Never in my forty years of existence had I ached for a man like I did right then.

Quinn broke off our kiss, shoving me behind him protectively.

Startled, I sputtered, "What…"

"Stay here," he ordered. "And no matter what you see or hear, don't approach." He strode off toward Brody and Jasper, who were at the far end of the club, holding back an irate Prudence. When Quinn arrived in front of the trio, Jasper and Brody walked away.

With his back facing me, Quinn was speaking with Prudence, whose short, skintight dress barely contained her huge breasts.

I tilted my head as I tried to hear what they were talking about, but between the music and distance, it was a lost cause.

"What a stalker," Nyx remarked.

Startled, I looked at her with wide eyes. "God, you're like some type of crazy ninja. You need to wear a freaking bell."

"Look at her." Nyx pointed in Prudence's direction. "She's making a fool of herself again. Quinn will handle her. Let's head back to the bar, have more shots, and wait for this ugliness with Prudence to be over." She walked away.

I was about to follow Nyx when I heard Prudence hiss, "Why her?"

Impossible.

There was no way in hell I heard what Prudence said, given the loud music and my distance from the duo.

"Prudence. Enough!" Quinn's voice was low, but I could hear the warning in his menacing tone. "Go home."

"But what about us?" Prudence whined.

"There was never any us," Quinn said. "I was crystal clear before and after I slept with you. I'm not claiming you."

"Don't say that," Prudence begged, stepping closer to Quinn. She reached out a hand to caress the side of his face.

I tightened my lips, fighting the urge to snarl. Every sense in my body heightened, incensed that Prudence had touched Quinn.

He grabbed Prudence's hand, tugging it from his face. "Don't."

Before I knew what I was doing, I made a beeline for my target. Prudence.

A loud growl erupted from my mouth. Quinn and Prudence both looked in my direction. Many eyes in the saloon locked on to me.

I blinked and shook my head, embarrassed by the attention.

What the fuck is wrong with me?

I'm acting like some feral animal, raring to fight over who gets to mate with Quinn.

How the hell did I become that woman?

The crazy chick about to stomp the ass of a woman because she touched a man who wasn't even hers?

He's ours, an animallike female voice declared.

I panned my eyes around, trying to figure out who was speaking. No one was near me.

Release me from my cage, and I'll take care of that she-bitch, the voice instructed.

Oh God! Her voice is inside my head. My inner animal had awoken and wanted to put the smackdown on Prudence.

Not good. What if I shifted?

I had no clue how and if I could control my animal.

My heart raced as I turned to get the fuck out of the club and rethink my life choices.

"Get back here, bitch!" Prudence yelled.

"Prudence!" Quinn barked. "One more word…"

I spun back around, knowing I was being addressed. Prudence was standing only inches from me. Quinn raced over, blocking Prudence from me.

I tried to sidestep him.

He blocked me again.

"Move, Quinn," I hissed. I didn't need him to fight my battles.

"No."

"Yes. Quinn, move so that I can wipe the floor with your weak-ass hybrid," Prudence taunted.

My skin prickled, and something wild and vicious arose within me before a deep-throated pulsing sound erupted from my mouth.

Quinn glanced over his shoulder at me. Whatever he saw on my face, he definitely didn't want to fuck with. He moved out of my way but still hovered by my side.

Prudence advanced, but I stood my ground. "He'll tire of you, hybrid, and come right back to me."

"I doubt it," I replied easily, fighting the urge to cunt-punt her across the saloon. *Don't do it, Imani,* I warned myself.

Prudence smirked, swiveling her head to Quinn. "Seriously, Quinn? You're picking this pathetic stray mutt over me?"

The words *stray mutt* hit me right in the gut, unearthing all the horrible, hurtful names my foster parents used to call me.

My inner beast rattled her cage.

"What did you call me?" I asked in a voice that was barely human.

Nyx barreled up to Prudence. "Get out, you—"

"Fuck off, witch." Prudence slapped Nyx so hard across the face that I could hear the loud crack over the music.

"Oh, hell no!" I yelled before smacking Prudence.

I blinked when I saw the deep claw marks across Prudence's cheek. My heart raced at the sight of black claws extending from my fingers.

"Oh my God," I whispered. "What's happening to me?"

Prudence touched a hand to her bloody cheek. "You bitch," she growled before lunging at me.

Quinn caught Prudence midleap and eased her back. "Touch Imani and you die." His expression was murderous.

Freya flashed over to Nyx, grabbing her while examining her swollen face. Freya's expression morphed into a mask of pure fury. "Prudence, get the fuck out of my saloon before I turn you into a toad."

Ignoring Freya, Prudence shouted at me. "You think that you're untouchable, but you're not, hybrid. I demand a duel." Her lips curved upward.

The crowd gasped.

I lifted my brows in confusion. "Duel?" She wants to fight with deadly weapons?

"No!" both Quinn and Freya yelled in unison.

"I demand vengeance." Prudence glared at him and then at me. "The hybrid drew first blood. I want her blood as payment."

"Blood?" My brows crinkled. "What is she talking about?"

"She's a hybrid," Quinn said to Prudence. "A duel only applies to full-blood shifters."

Prudence spun away from Quinn, turning to face the crowd of interested partiers, which had grown larger.

"I demand a duel with this coward!" Prudence's voice was loud and angry.

"Bring it on," I replied, not even sure what I was signing up for.

Quinn stepped in front of me. "And I said no!"

Blocked by Quinn, I could only hear Prudence's mocking laugh. I tried to step around him, but it was almost as if he was in my head, stepping to the left or right when I did, effectively hiding me.

"It's shifter law, Quinn, and your hybrid has shifter blood."

Jasper and Brody suddenly flanked me. I looked over at both of them, but they were staring at Prudence, their expressions grim.

What the hell is happening?

"She hasn't shifted into her beast yet," Quinn contended. "A full-blood dueling against a hybrid is the equivalent of bringing a gun to a knife fight."

The crowd nodded in agreement.

Prudence tapped her lip coyly. "How about if I agree to fight only in my human form?"

"Like I trust anything you say," Quinn retorted.

"Take it or leave it, Quinn," Prudence answered.

"Leave it," he barked. "Imani's not fighting. She's not one of us. Our laws don't apply to her."

I frowned, pissed that they were talking about me like I wasn't even there.

"But they apply to you, and she's yours," Prudence pointed out. "Or do you deny that, Quinn?" She smiled smugly.

His voice was loud when he spoke. "Imani is my fated mate. You and everyone in this fucking place would do well to remember that." Quinn abruptly dismissed Prudence, turning to face me. His hand was suddenly around my waist as he half dragged me toward the entrance.

"Quinn!" Prudence yelled. "You and your mate better show up at midnight on Sunday."

Confused, I looked back to see Freya, Nyx, Jasper, and Brody facing off with Prudence.

"Quinn?" I ventured.

"Not now, Imani," he snapped as we stepped out into the crisp night air.

CHAPTER 26
QUINN

Pissed, I was still sitting in my truck in front of the saloon.

Every time I thought about what had just happened, I wanted to slam my fist into the dashboard.

Prudence had goaded Imani into drawing first blood, giving her the right to demand Imani's blood as retribution in a duel—a bloody fight between shifters.

I stole a glance at Imani, remembering how her hands had shifted into claws, but she still hadn't fully shifted into her beast. There was no way Imani could beat Prudence in a duel. I'd figure out how to deal with Prudence tomorrow.

Imani's mine. My fated mate. Her changed eyes had confirmed what I already knew. And I'd kill anyone and anything that tried to hurt her.

Finally calm enough to focus on Imani, I glanced over to find her nibbling on her bottom lip, staring at me.

"Imani," I started. "I'm sorry—"

She cut me off. "What's a duel?"

"It's nothing."

She snorted and murmured under her breath, "Great, more secrets the hybrid can't know."

"It's not a secret."

"So tell me what it is." She glared at me with eyes transformed to amber—a sure sign that her inner beast had acknowledged me as Imani's mate.

"Are you sure you want to know?" I demanded.

"Yes, dammit. I want to know."

I gripped the steering so hard, I thought I'd break it off. "It's an act of vengeance between two shifters," I disclosed.

Confusion clouded her gaze. "And that means what? A fight with weapons?"

"No. It's a combat fight, animal against animal."

Her eyes widened. "But Prudence is a wolf-shifter."

"A full-blood wolf-shifter." I exhaled loudly. "Believe me, Prudence wants this fight for more than retribution. She thinks this is a stepping-stone to becoming my mate and alpha female of my pack and town."

"And what do you want?"

"You know what I want." I touched her thigh.

She shoved my hand off her. "Your fuck buddy Prudence."

"Let's get this shit out in the open."

"Let's." Her eyes narrowed.

"I slept with Prudence once. The night of my alpha challenge against Sam. And for full transparency, Prudence and I both agreed it was just sex. But with Prudence, nothing is what it appears to be."

She eyed me suspiciously. "So she's in love after having sex with you once?"

I grabbed her hand. "This has nothing to do with love," I said. She pulled her hand away. "Prudence wants power over my pack and this town. She wants to be alpha female, and that will never happen.

"I want you. My fated mate. Someone to love and who will love me in return. I want my soul mate, not a female who views me as another step closer to power." I clenched and unclenched my fists. "Even though I'd given up on the possibility of finding my mate, I'd never stopped hoping, even in the bleakest of times when my animal threatened to send me feral, that I'd find her." I stared at her with my heart racing. "You are more than I'd hoped for."

She sighed. "Oh, Quinn." She pressed her palm against my cheek, and my inner beast growled with pleasure.

"You are my fated mate, Imani." I turned my head, pressing a kiss against her palm. "Everything about you calls to me. Your scent, inner and outer beauty. Your strength and intellect. And if that's not enough proof that you're my fated mate, our eyes turned amber on the dance floor, which is a sign of the truthfulness of our match. It's nature's way of preparing us for the mating lust that will soon be upon us."

"Quinn." She pulled her trembling fingers away. "I'm scared."

My heart raced. "Imani, my beast and I would never physically hurt you."

"I know that." She licked her lips. "I'm afraid of you breaking my heart. I could deal with anything but that."

"I would never do that, Imani. I know that our ways, the shifter ways, are hard for you to understand, but when we give our heart and love, it's forever. We do not profess love and devotion when it is not true."

I placed my hand over her heart. "Try to put your fear aside. Trust what your mind is saying. You are mine. I know this. But if you need time for me to prove my worthiness as your mate, then I will do so."

"I don't need time, Quinn. I need you to be honest with me, even if you think that the weirdness in this town or shifter ways will scare the shit out of me."

I nodded. "Okay. I will do that."

"Now let's talk about my duel with the she-bitch."

"The duel is not happening," I fumed.

"Why not?"

"Because a hybrid that's never shifted is no match against a full-blood wolf-shifter like Prudence," I explained.

She stiffened. "So you're already predicting I'll lose without giving me a chance?"

"Yes."

"Fuck you, Quinn." She opened the door, hopping out of my truck with a door slam.

"Dammit!" I yelled, exiting my vehicle and storming after her. "Where the hell are you going?"

"Don't know. Don't care."

I caught up with her, matching her strides. "What the hell is the matter with you, woman?"

She stopped with her hands on her hips. "You!"

"What did I do now?" I demanded.

"We just agreed that we're fated mates."

"I agreed, but you didn't tell me how you feel," I countered.

"Ugh." She threw her hands up in the air. "You are so frustrating, Alpha."

"Well?" I needed to hear her feelings.

"You are mine. And I am yours. And I don't commit to relationships, so this is epic for me. I don't share because I'm greedy as hell. So know this right now—it's me and you and no fucking around with anyone but me."

"Agreed." I traced a finger across her cheek.

"Now let's get back to the duel. Why the fuck did you tell Prudence that I'm not a shifter and shifter laws don't apply to me?"

I frowned. "I already told you why. You don't have the fighting skills to take on Prudence."

"So I'm nothing but a weak hybrid who's not strong enough to stand toe-to-toe with a wolf-shifter?" She exploded.

"Imani...," I started.

"Don't Imani me." She poked me in the chest. "Right now I want to punch you in the face so bad I can practically taste it." She stormed away again. "Crazy alpha!" she screamed, throwing her hands in the air.

I took off after her again. When I caught up with her, I said, "I don't know why you're so angry."

"Because all my life, I've been underestimated and underappreciated. And just when I thought I'd found a man who respected and accepted me as his equal, you went and announced to the whole fucking saloon that I'm nothing but a weak hybrid." She stopped and stared at me. "Now I don't stand a chance in hell of being respected or accepted in Black Forest."

My mind processed what she'd said. *Fuck! She's right.*

As my mate, Imani would have no choice but to fight.

If she didn't, she'd have a target on her back for the rest of her life.

This was a damned if she did and damned if she didn't situation. But the thought of her fighting Prudence chilled me to the bone.

"So I'm wrong for wanting to protect you?" I demanded.

"Quinn." She tilted her head and studied me. "I get that you're worried about me. But supporting me on this duel topic is very important to me."

She huffed. "Not once did you ask whether I could fight. Well, I can. All my life, I've had to fight. Battle the kids at school because they thought it was fun to kick the shit out of my ass every day because I was the weird girl who didn't have any friends. Fight the kids at every foster home because there was a pecking order, and I was always the loner and runt in the house. Fight to be taken seriously in the male-dominated food industry because I was the only female chef in the kitchen." It hurt my heart that she'd had it so bad growing up and to this day.

"Darling, I didn't know."

"That's why I'm telling you." She grabbed my hand, threading her fingers through mine. "I'm sharing a piece of me that still hurts me to the core. I'm revealing the chink in my armor because I know you won't abuse my trust in you."

Her trust and belief in me were humbling. "Never."

"Then trust me to hold my own against Prudence. Trust that I can stand by your side as your equal. Because if you don't believe in me, then I don't want to be in your life at all." She released my hand.

I stared at her, open-mouthed. It felt as if she'd dug a claw into my stomach and had dragged out my innards.

I swallowed past a sudden tightness in my throat. "Having someone like you in my life is new territory for me, and I don't know how to handle it." I took a deep breath to steady myself. "You're everything I need but never expected."

The tiniest smile ghosted onto her lips. "And what about what I need, Quinn?"

"I won't clip your wings, Imani. You have my full support on the duel."

Seconds passed with us silently staring at each other.

I brushed a finger across her cheek. "You're more woman than I deserve."

She smiled. "Remember that thought when I'm annoying the shit out of you, which I do a lot."

I laughed. "Come here, woman." Wrapping my arms around her, I pressed my body to every part of her. Her arms encircled my waist. Our kiss started off hot and heavy and didn't ease up. My chest rumbled, which meant that both man and beast were happy.

Imani was mine, and I was hers, and if the townsfolk of Black Forest couldn't handle that future, I didn't give a shit.

I lifted her off her feet, holding her even tighter. She wrapped her legs around my waist.

"Damn," I muttered against her mouth.

"Yes, damn."

She nuzzled my cheek, and I fought back a grin.

I kissed the tip of her nose. "Let's go home."

"Okay, Alpha." She unwrapped her legs to stand.

I grabbed her hand, leading her back to my truck as sheets of icy rain started falling over us.

CHAPTER 27
IMANI

Quinn pulled up to his ranch, then stepped out of his truck. I watched as he strode around to open my door. When he took my hand, I inhaled, feeling the electricity that seemed to pour from his skin to mine as he escorted me inside his home.

Wasting no time, Quinn led me upstairs, bypassing the guest room I'd slept in. Pushing open the door to another room that I assumed was his bedroom, he flipped on the light with one hand, illuminating the space.

I slid my hands around his waist, pressing into his body, feeling the rippling muscles beneath his shirt.

I tugged at his shirt. "Take this off," I demanded.

His eyes glowed amber when he said, "You first."

Stepping back, I kicked off my shoes, then stripped down, leaving only my panties on.

"Do you like what you see?" I teased.

"Yes," he growled before lifting me off the floor. Gasping with pleasure, I locked my legs around his waist, my arms around his neck as he slid his hand along my bare thigh, then up my back.

I tightened my grip on his neck, nipping at his bottom lip hard, and was rewarded with a deep moan before he devoured my mouth and carried me across his large bedroom. I sucked at his tongue while he followed me down on his massive bed.

He broke off our kiss as I frantically tugged at his shirt.

I longed to see him naked again.

I burned to run my fingers along his taut skin and muscles.

I wanted to suck and taste him.

"Shirt off," I ordered.

Quinn tugged off the garment to reveal the solid mass of his chest. He was tight and toned in every way possible. I reached out with a finger, tracing the hardness of his arms. Under my touch, he tensed. His eyes closed, and his breath came fast. A wicked smile touched my lips as I pushed onto an elbow, running my tongue over his flat nipple.

He pinned me against the bed, removing and tossing my panties aside. When Quinn kissed me again, I grabbed the back of his head. The hardness of his chest crushed my full breasts, and his hips nestled between my spread legs. His lips moved down my neck, licking and sucking at pleasure points before making their way to my nipples.

"Fuck," I groaned as he flicked his tongue rapidly over my nipple before circling the peak and then lightly nipping at it. He licked down the valley of my breasts to my navel, where he circled the little indentation. The bed shifted, and my eyes opened. He was standing at the foot of the bed, his features harsh yet controlled.

"Quinn?"

A squeal escaped my lips when he locked his hand on to my ankle, sliding me down the bed. He pulled once more until my hips were at the bed's edge, and he spread my legs before him like a decadent feast.

His amber eyes locked on mine as he palmed my pussy.

Nibbling my bottom lip, I arched into his hand. Feeling naughty, I spread my legs wider, exposing my passionate sex.

"Imani, you are perfection."

Kneeling for better access, he leaned forward, inhaling my

pulsating cunt before his tongue touched my slit, sending me careening into an orgasm. Pushing my legs farther apart, he attacked my pussy with a ravenous vengeance, as if he couldn't get enough of my taste.

Coming down from my last orgasm, I watched as Quinn took off his jeans in one fluid motion. He was commando. My mouth watered, staring at the wide, long cock springing up from a nest of black hair at his thighs.

Damn, he's deliciously big.

His cock seemed to grow even larger the longer I stared. He strode over to the nightstand, taking out a roll of condoms. Ripping off a square, he opened it, sheathing his cock. When he came back to the bed, he had his hands under my armpits, pulling me farther up the bed, to the center of the large mattress.

"Quinn, it's been a long time since I've been with a man."

He traced a finger across my lips as he reached down with the other hand to capture a soft breast. I moaned, my lips parting slightly and tongue darting out to lick at his finger.

"I'll take it slow." His gravelly voice sent vibrations of lust throughout my body. "I would rather kill myself than hurt you. Do you believe me?"

"Yes," I whispered.

He nudged my thighs apart and settled between them. His hands went to my face as he leaned down and kissed my lips. His tongue caressed mine. My nails dragged along his skin as I clutched at him, arching into the hard length that rubbed against my pussy.

He growled, burying his face into my neck. I moaned as he sucked at my neck and cried out when he slid his finger into me. My hips rose off the bed to meet it as it moved within me. He inserted another, and I whimpered as my walls stretched to accommodate it.

"That's it, darling. Just like that." His voice was husky as his fingers prepared me for his invasion. I was approaching another orgasm when his fingers slipped free from my body and his hard cock pressed against me. He rubbed his thick length along my slit, teasing me seductively.

I slid my hand into his hair. He growled, sounding wild, but I didn't care. Surging forward, he impaled me on his enormous length. I jerked back before forcing myself to relax. He slid deeper, finally sheathed inside me.

God, he feels so good.

He held himself still for a few seconds, then he moved, pulling back slowly, only to slide deep at the same pace. I was so wet and ready for him that, despite my tightness, he moved inside smoothly. Reaching down, he grabbed my leg, pushing it out to the side before raising it by the knee. Another inch of him slipped into my body, and I cried out with pleasure.

Quinn moved faster, quickening his pace as he pushed me toward another orgasm. Arching off the bed, I came hard, collapsing right after, sweaty and worn out. Not finished with me, he pulled out of my body and flipped me onto my belly. Reaching under me, he lifted me until I was on my knees. I moaned, leaning my head back against his shoulder.

With one arm holding me up, Quinn nipped my neck and shoulders and kissed each little bite after. He brought his other hand down to my center and danced his fingers over my sensitive nub.

I moaned low when he lightly pinched me with his fingers before turning his hands to my breasts. After tugging at my nipples, he kissed my shoulder, then my spine, before he released my breasts and trailed kisses down to the dip in my back. He pushed at my shoulder, and I went forward, my hands against the mattress.

Quinn growled. One look over my shoulder showed me I'd turned him on with the sight of me on my knees before him. His lips parted, revealing his lengthened canines.

The air crackled around us, and I felt a burst of renewed energy shoot through me. Strong hands gripped my waist, and I pushed back against air, whimpering in frustration.

A scream tore from my throat as his length parted my folds in one quick thrust. One hand gripped my waist as the other tangled in my hair. I cried out, feeling a combination of delicious pain and pleasure as he thrust against me, his sweat-slicked body rocking against mine as his pace increased.

"I will be the only one to have you, Imani. Only me. Do you accept me as your mate?"

I nodded frantically. "Yes. Only you."

His thrusts grew even stronger, his body slapping against mine so powerfully that the king-sized bed shook. My hands caught fistfuls of sheet as I pushed back against him, feeling my body burn with the need to release.

"Like that, Imani?"

"Yes. More. Harder. Faster."

He came down against my back as he pressed his hands into the mattress on either side of me. Turning my head, I blinked when I saw the color of his eyes.

"Um, Quinn. Your eyes are amber again."

"And so are yours, darling."

I gasped as he went deep.

"You are mine, Quinn. My mate."

"Always and forever, Imani."

A sharp pain lanced my shoulder, and my knees buckled. His arm was below my belly, holding me up while a burn started at my shoulder.

Quinn quickened his pace, and something strange erupted inside me. Something much fiercer had taken over my inner beast. He pushed against me again, and I rocked back into him frantically. A soft growl escaped my lips, and then a cry, a keening, high-pitched sound, left my lips.

"Take me, Quinn. Take me completely."

A strangled shout came from him as he pushed forward wildly, his cock increasing in girth as he came. My eyes widened when my body demanded more of him. He reared back and pushed forward again, and my body stretched further as it tried to accommodate him. Another hard thrust resulted in my broken cry; he was sheathed in my body. Heat pulsed through my core.

My body began shaking, quivering, coming.

I heard a feral snarl, followed by a growl from Quinn. My body shook violently, and something inside me unlocked. There was no other way to describe it. The world erupted into sound. My inner beast howled in my head, rain beating against the window, Quinn's harsh breathing in my ear.

My breath was calming when my inner beast announced, *Now I am whole and happy.*

Quinn wrapped his arm around my belly as he carefully lowered us onto our sides. He was still inside me, still hard.

"More," I demanded.

"Mine," he replied.

CHAPTER 28
IMANI

The next morning, I awoke to the sound of sniffing and Quinn's nose pressed against my neck. "What are you doing, Quinn?" My body was on fire. I kicked at the stifling sheets.

"Your scent has changed." He prowled over me, staring at me with intense eyes.

I was burning up and in a wicked state of arousal. "Is that your polite way of saying it's time for a shower?"

"No." He pushed my legs apart, pressing his hard cock against my womanhood.

"Then what?" I slid my hands around his neck, pulling him closer and loving the feel of his skin against mine.

He had an amused expression on his face. "You're going into heat, mate."

"Um, what?" I croaked. I vaguely remembered Piper, Nyx, and Freya discussing the topic, but right now, with the tornado of heat engulfing my body, the finer details of the discussion had escaped my head.

"It's when a mated female is in a heightened sense of arousal that only her mate can satisfy."

My heart was racing from the anxiety of going into heat. "And how long is this heat going to last?"

"At least a couple of days," he explained.

"Not acceptable." I shoved him playfully. "We need to put this heat thing on hold. I have to help Piper with the B and B, and I have a duel."

He laughed. "Put your heat on hold?"

I grunted. "Yes."

"Good luck with that," he muttered.

"You'd be amazed at what I can do if I put my mind to it," I boasted.

"Imani, you can't schedule going into heat. It just happens naturally."

"Watch me." I eyed him pointedly. "Move it, Alpha. I have to get ready for work."

"Okay." He rolled over onto his back, taking the sheets with him.

I moaned as his decadent scent washed over to me. "Oh hell," I grumbled when the sharp need to fuck stabbed me. Rolling over, I pushed myself onto my hands and knees, ready for him to take me again.

He slapped my butt. "Love your ass." He hopped off the bed. "See you in the shower," he said, moving around the bed and heading toward the bathroom.

Impatiently wiggling my butt, I hissed, "Get your ass back over here, Quinn."

He walked over to my side of the bed and stood there eyeing me. "What about work?"

"Fuck me," I growled.

"What's the magic word?"

"Now!" I answered.

He crossed his arms. "Try again."

"Please." I gritted my teeth when another wave of heat threatened to consume me.

"Now that you asked politely..." He opened a condom foil, sheathing his cock. Moving behind me, he massaged my buttocks. "You have the most beautiful ass," he rumbled.

He slid his fingers down the crack between my cheeks, touching my folds so intimately I gasped.

"Fuck. You're so wet for me."

He glided his fingers through my wetness over and over until I squirmed uncontrollably. The air was sultry around us as his hands gripped my waist, and he eased his cock into me smoothly.

"Oh," I cried out with pleasure as one of his hands gripped my hair, with the other wrapped around my waist. He rocked his body into mine. Our slick bodies moved in perfect synchrony, with a strong, magnetic energy encircling us.

"Don't stop," I begged as I gripped the bedsheets.

Growling, he clutched the sides of my hips. He reared back and pushed forward. Every inch of him was now sheathed inside me. My body shuddered, legs quivered, and core pulsed.

"I would never leave you wanting, mate," he promised roughly, thrusting faster.

"I'm going to come," I wailed.

"Not until I allow you."

His body slapped against mine ruthlessly. I rocked back into him, taking everything he had to give.

"Quinn, please." My body burned for sweet release.

"Come. Now!"

A strangled shout escaped my lips before I felt the orgasm ripping up my spine, tearing through my limbs.

"Quinn!" I shouted as I felt his cock pulse. My cunt contracted, milking him as both of us crested.

He kissed me on the shoulder before pulling me farther up on the bed.

"Shit. That was fucking hot," he whispered against my lips, clutching my body against his.

"Hell yes, it was." I smiled even as another wave of lust whipped through my body. "Get on your back, Alpha. It's time for round two."

~

Moonlight spread across the bed, and I woke up exhausted after dealing with unbearable heat and multiple rounds of fucking. My temperature wasn't as hot as it was yesterday morning, but the urge for sex was still persistent.

Rolling over, I grabbed my cell, checking out the time. It was midnight. I moaned, rubbing my thighs together. I needed him inside me again.

"Quinn," I moaned, rolling onto my back.

He snapped open his eyes before grabbing a condom, sheathing his cock, and rolling onto me.

"Yes," I hissed as his thick staff pushed into me. Hiking my legs around his waist, I moaned as his thrusts got wild and rough, which was exactly what I craved. An orgasm raced through me as he bit my neck and came. Both of us were tired and breathy. He rolled onto his side, taking me with him, cradling my back against his chest.

"Quinn, where are the sheets? I'm freezing."

Reaching down to the floor for the bedding, he covered us.

"What day is it?" I mumbled.

"Saturday." He sniffed my neck. "The scent is fading. You're coming out of heat. In a few hours, you'll be through it."

"Yay," I croaked. "How often does this heat thingy happen?"

"It's common for newly mated females to go into heat multiple times in the first six months after being claimed."

"I guess we're going to be real busy," I replied.

"Yes, mate. We are," he whispered in my ear before pulling me against him.

CHAPTER 29
IMANI

It was Sunday, and Quinn had gotten up early, serving me a delicious breakfast in bed before leaving me to take care of ranch business.

I'd slept for hours before getting up at three. I wanted desperately to hop into the shower, but before Quinn left, he'd asked me not to take a shower. He wanted his scent all over me. When I balked at his crazy request, he said, "It's a wolf thing. It tells Others you're mated and claimed."

"The things I do for this man," I grumped while hopping out of bed, heading to the bathroom to brush my teeth and wash my face.

When I got out of the bathroom, I smiled when I saw my luggage placed in a corner of the room. Opening up my bag, I pulled out a pair of black leggings, socks, lingerie, a T-shirt, and a long-sleeved fitted shirt. My attire would provide enough coverage and protection during my fight with Prudence. Quickly donning everything, I pulled on a pair of sneakers and then gathered my hair into a high ponytail before heading downstairs and following the sounds of loud voices.

"Quinn, we need to talk some sense into her!" Piper yelled.

"Been there," Quinn said. "Done that. Imani's mind is set on fighting Prudence. And I'm going to support her."

I strolled into the kitchen and saw everyone either seated or standing around the huge kitchen island. Talking ceased. All heads—Piper, Nyx, Freya, Jasper, Brody, Mack, Emmett, Rhett, and Quinn—turned to stare at me.

"Hello," I chirped.

The kitchen was so silent that I could hear a pin drop.

I walked over to the coffeepot, pouring myself a cup.

Quinn strode over to me, giving me a long, deep kiss before pulling back to cup my face. "How are you feeling, mate?"

"Wonderful." Stepping back, I took a sip of coffee. "So where is the location of my duel tonight?"

He stared at me long and hard, as if willing me to drop the topic, but I only returned his stare steadily.

"Main Square," he grunted. "Eight tonight."

"Great," I replied. "I'm ready."

"Okay, if no one will say it, I will," Mack growled. "This is crazy." He stared at me. "Imani, you can't fight Prudence."

"I can and I will," I replied before taking another sip of coffee. I didn't provoke this duel drama; Prudence did, and all because she couldn't take being rejected by Quinn.

"I love it," Freya said. "She's already acting like an alpha female."

Piper rolled her eyes. "You ain't saying anything we don't already know."

"I think Imani can beat her," Nyx chimed in, giving me a thumbs-up.

"No one asked you, Nyx," Brody said, which started a fresh round of arguing between Nyx and Brody, then between Mack and Nyx, then with all three.

Quinn crossed his beefy arms, staring at them like there were a bunch of unruly kids he was seconds away from putting in time-out.

Shit. This is a circus.

"This is bullshit," Rhett shouted.

"No," Emmett snapped. "What's bullshit is that Prudence doesn't even live in this fucking town."

"I second that," Freya shouted.

"Will everyone just calm the hell down?" Jasper demanded.

"I can't take all this screaming." Piper rubbed her temple. "Y'all are giving me a headache."

Quinn whistled loudly, cutting them off.

"So who's hungry?" I asked.

They all looked at me like I'd lost my mind, but as an executive chef, I knew that food brought people together.

"Uh, darling...," Quinn started.

Ignoring him, I said, "Everyone get your ass up. It's time to pull your weight by helping me cook up a meal."

Freya fluffed her bouncy hair. "Sweetie, I don't cook."

"Imani," Nyx said, "believe me, you don't want her cooking. She's horrible at it."

Freya gently slapped Nyx on the back of her head. "Oh, hush up. You didn't starve growing up."

Nyx snorted. "We had takeout so much I thought the deliverymen were your boyfriends."

I pointed at Freya. "You're in charge of making fresh lemonade." I jabbed a finger at the lemons in the basket on the counter. "Twelve lemons. Cut them in half and squeeze them like it's the ass of one of your male strippers."

"Yummy," Freya said. "There was this stripper..."

"Freya?" I snapped my fingers. "Focus please. Squeeze the juice into that huge jug on the top shelf."

Freya grumbled as she washed her hands before getting to work.

"Put me to work," Piper said.

"Can you set the table?" I asked.

"Yes. On it." She grinned before hustling away.

I eyed Quinn. "Do you have cooked ham?"

"Of course," he answered. "It's in the refrigerator."

I rubbed my hands together like a mad scientist. "Now for my scalloped potatoes and ham dish. I'm going to need lots of potatoes. Rhett and Mack." I pointed to the basket full. "Slice them real thin. The thinner, the better."

They got up and did as told.

"Hop to it, Sheriff and Deputy," Nyx said.

I gave her the stink eye. "Do you want to eat?"

"Of course. I've had your cooking, and it's delicious."

"Then stop goading them and preheat the top oven to 375. After that, get the cooked ham out of the refrigerator and dice it," I ordered.

"Yes, ma'am." She gave me a mock salute before getting on task.

Jasper laughed before pulling out his cell and texting.

"Cell down, Jasper," I demanded. "You have work to do. Chop up some onions and mince the garlic."

He grumbled something about stinky onions but did what I said.

I eyed Quinn. "You have any rib eye steaks?"

He arched a brow. "Darling, no self-respecting shifter wouldn't."

"Great. Take out enough for everyone. Lay them on sheet pans, sprinkling each side with pepper and salt."

He walked up to me. "We all see what you're doing."

I batted my eyes prettily. "And what's that?"

"Using food to calm the savage beast." He gave me a quick kiss. "Great job."

"I know." I swatted his ass. "Now get those steaks prepped."

"Yes, mate." He winked at me before walking over to the refrigerator.

"Emmett, you're on biscuit duty," I directed. "There are frozen biscuits in the freezer. Preheat the bottom oven to 350."

"Got it," Emmett answered.

"Brody. We'll need broccoli. Also chop up some tomatoes for the salad. Thanks."

"On it," Brody replied.

Sipping my now-lukewarm coffee, I watched everyone concentrating on his or her assignment. The kitchen was massive, so they all had their own work area.

I exhaled. The sounds of chopping and prepping were heaven compared to their bickering. Of course, I was under no illusion that their minds weren't still on my duel tonight, but at least I'd defused the tension in the kitchen.

Draining my cup, I put it in the sink before pulling a baking dish from the cabinet. I got a block of butter out of the refrigerator, carrying both items over to Rhett.

With rolled-up sleeves, he sliced the potatoes. "How do they look?" he asked.

"Perfection," I said, placing the butter and baking dish on the counter next to him. "Butter the dish generously."

I turned to Mack. "And Mack. Can you layer the slices inside the dish?"

"No problem," Mack replied.

"Mack?" I ventured.

"Yes?"

"Why are you so worried about me fighting Prudence?"

There was no tension in his voice when he answered. "Because I don't want you to lose or get hurt."

"Well then, I won't lose," I said simply. I wasn't kidding when I said that I knew how to fight. I'd learned the basics of fighting skills from the school of hard knocks—aka fighting every day in the schoolyard—but when I'd reached adulthood, I'd hired a retired professional MMA fighter to train me.

"Well, I, for one, don't give a shit if you lose," Quinn groused. "You're my mate, and I don't want you getting hurt or killed."

I sauntered over to him, cupping his cheek. "Remember our conversation about trust?"

He nuzzled my hand. "Yes."

"Then trust me, okay?"

He nodded.

Satisfied, I strode over to get a skillet, placing it on the stove. "Rhett, give me a high-level duel summary." I turned the heat to medium.

Rhett dumped a handful of sliced potatoes into a large bowl. "It's a refereed fight."

"Jasper," I called. "Please bring me those onions you chopped."

Jasper walked over with a bowl of onions and said, "In a duel, the two individuals fight to first blood or, depending on the severity of the offense, sometimes to the death."

"Death?" I queried softly, adding butter and onions to the large skillet that was now hot.

"Yes," Jasper replied.

"And whoever draws blood first claims victory," Rhett added. "But with most duels, first blood happens fast because the fight is quick."

"But this duel is different," Brody chimed in.

"Why?" I asked.

"Because Prudence wants to fight to the death," Nyx informed me.

I stiffened, pissed at how serious Prudence would let this fight get. "What a psycho bitch." I sprinkled flour over the onions and whisked them together.

Freya nodded. "Yes, she is."

"Imani," Emmett said. "None of us will think less of you if you don't fight Prudence."

"I know that, Emmett," I said. "But everyone in this room knows that if I don't fight Prudence, that would be like putting a target on my back. There's no way in hell I'm going to live my life in this town having to look over my shoulder every day. I have to take a stand. Show Prudence that I'm not to be fucked with." When I was young, I learned that the only way to stop a bully was by not backing down. "Now any more rules?"

"Yes," Quinn said grimly. "Prudence agreed to no shifting,

but I don't trust her to hold true to that agreement. If she shifts, she'll kill you, and I won't let that happen. I'll intervene, and I don't give a shit that the shifter laws say I can't."

"Let's hope it doesn't come to that," I replied, continuing to cook the onion-flour mixture until golden brown. "What else?"

Brody's eyes narrowed. "The loser has to show their belly to the winner, and the winner can either show mercy or kill the loser."

"It's a sign of submission," Freya clarified, still squeezing lemons.

"Got it," I replied, stirring in half-and-half and milk and then whisking it around.

They all stared at me with worried eyes.

I turned to face them head-on. "Come on, guys. Think positive."

"How can we?" Piper remarked. "You can die out there tonight."

"I know that." I sighed heavily. "And I'm not being cavalier about that possibility. The thought of being killed by Prudence is frightening, but this is my home and town now." I extended a hand to Quinn, who entwined his fingers with mine, pulling me to his side. "I have a man I adore and who adores me."

"You're damn right," he responded.

I continued, "I have friends and a pack who are now my family."

Everyone nodded.

"And don't you forget that," Emmett rumbled.

"I won't," I replied. "And that's why I'm not walking away from everything I dreamed of but didn't think I'd ever have. Family." I glanced around to each one of them. "So what I need the most right now is my family to trust me when I say that I'm going to destroy that crazy hag tonight. Do you trust me?"

The responses came swiftly. "Yes." "Always." Along with nods.

"Well, that's all I need," I said. "Now let's finish prepping dinner so I can get to cooking."

Everyone grinned before getting back to his or her task. Nyx turned on music. Brody pulled out bottles of beer. Piper took out glasses. I smiled at what was now turning into a celebration of life and being together with the genuine family I'd been waiting for all my life.

Quinn turned me to face him. "Did I tell you you're the best thing to happen to me?"

"Yes." I reached up, running my fingers through his hair. "But I will not stop you from saying it again."

"Imani, you're the best fucking thing to happen to me." He nipped my bottom lip.

"Ditto, shifter. Ditto."

CHAPTER 30
IMANI

My nerves were a mess when Quinn drove up to the front of the town hall building and parked.

"Relax," he said, resting his palm against my thigh.

"Okay." I took a deep, calming breath.

"You ready?"

I nodded.

"Let's go." He squeezed my leg.

He opened the driver's door, striding around to open my door. Hopping out, I watched the rest of the pack, plus Freya and Nyx, getting out of their vehicles.

Quinn and I strode toward the open grass field with the pack, Freya and Nyx following.

"Focus on what you have to do," Quinn instructed while rubbing small, comforting circles against the middle of my back. "Prudence will try to goad you. Don't let that happen."

"Got it."

"Bonnie, a council member, will officiate the duel. All the council members will be there and I'm sure the entire town. Remember, once we get to the field, walk ahead of me. This is a sign of strength, bravery, and that you stand strong as the alpha female of the Bane pack and this town."

"Okay." Adrenaline coursed through my veins in anticipation of the fight.

My eyes widened when we reached the crowded field. It seemed like everyone in Black Forest had shown up to witness my duel.

The boisterous crowd parted like the sea when I strode to the center of the field, leaving Quinn behind.

A lone statuesque woman with dark skin was standing there. "I am Bonnie," the woman said. "Good fighting, alpha female."

Quinn stepped to my right, near but not touching me.

Holding her arms above her head, Bonnie waited for the noise to die down and then said in a clear, even voice, "This duel has been called and answered." She lowered her hands to her sides. "Who calls this duel?" Bonnie demanded.

"I do," Prudence announced, shoving through the crowd with Sam trailing behind her.

"Sam, you even flinch at Imani," Quinn barked, "I'll rip your damn head off your shoulders."

Sam's eyes widened before he hightailed it into the throng.

I kept my focus on Prudence, almost snorting at her ridiculous outfit—bare feet and a metallic-gold one-piece spandex bodysuit that left nothing to the imagination. Meanwhile, my clothing was practical and comfortable for fighting—a fitted sleeveless tank top, black spandex leggings, and sneakers.

"And who answers this duel?" Bonnie asked, looking directly at me.

"I do," I said in a clear, loud voice. "Alpha female of the Bane pack and this town."

Bonnie nodded and dipped her head to me and then to Prudence.

"Whenever you're both ready," Bonnie declared, then promptly stepped back.

The spectators moved in unison to stand shoulder to shoulder, forming a wide circle that surrounded Prudence and me.

Quinn stepped behind me, tugging me so that my back

pressed against his chest. He pulled aside the strap of my tank top, biting down against the place he'd bitten me last night. Licking the spot, he eased the sting of pain.

"Fight well," he whispered in my ear, and then he left to join the circle.

"That mating bite means nothing," Prudence shrieked.

Apparently it did, because now she was pissed at Quinn's display of affection.

Prudence launched herself at me.

I dashed out of the way, and she landed in a crouch and then stood.

She lunged again; I sidestepped her again. My plan was to tire and frustrate Prudence before I whaled on her ass like she owed me money.

"Fight, bitch," Prudence scolded, cracking her neck left and right.

The crowd booed loudly.

"Oh, shut up, idiots," I snapped, glaring around at them.

But taking my eyes off Prudence was a mistake. She shoved me back, and I flew, landing hard on my ass.

Move! My inner animal instructed.

I attempted to scramble to my feet, but Prudence beat me to the punch by knocking me onto my back, straddling me.

"Let's see how much Quinn wants you once I've fucked up that pretty face of yours," Prudence bellowed, tearing at my face with long, manicured fingernails.

Every slice of her nails against my face felt like needles digging into my skin. I swung my arms, landing hard shots to Prudence's body. One blow was so hard that she wobbled back, giving me the opportunity to jump to my feet. Breathing hard from the exertion, I ran a hand over my cheek, feeling the welts where Prudence had gouged my flesh. My hand came away bloody. My face throbbed.

"You psycho cunt!" I shouted.

"Look who's not so pretty now," Prudence boasted, then began circling me.

My fingers tingled. Rage raced through my veins.

Let. Me. Out, my beast begged.

Prudence launched at me again. Pissed, I landed a hook square to her jaw. Capitalizing on her stunned expression, I put Prudence in a clinch and unloaded brutal knee strikes to her body. Prudence's body went slack, and I released the hold, watching her fall face-first onto the grass. *Timber!*

"Get the fuck up," I ordered. "I'm not done with you. You just released the kraken."

Prudence was injured, but somehow, she got the strength to leap to her feet, sending a hard kick to my belly. I doubled over from the blow, but the pain only fueled my rage. Straightening my body, I was ready to end this shit by putting my fist through her face.

I froze when Prudence let out a yell like a banshee. Her spandex ripped off her body, and black fur sprouted all over her face and limbs. The bitch shifted into a wolf.

The crowd yelled and clapped like they were at some damn football game.

"Holy shit," I hissed as the wolf charged, tail like a flag and hackles raised, heading straight for me.

"No!" I heard Quinn shout.

"Don't do it, Quinn!" Rhett yelled. "Let her fight."

I lifted my leg forward, extending it with force, using my hips to generate power. My push kick blasted the wolf back.

The audience made sounds of "oohs" and "aahs."

The wolf rose onto its hind legs. I twisted my body, delivering a roundhouse kick, sending her flying backward again.

The wolf growled before taking off on a full-tilt run in my direction. When she reached me, she lowered her body to the ground, fixing her eyes on me before rolling over and showing her belly.

Her wolf was submitting to me.

I stilled, processing my win, when the wolf flipped over and leaped up, closing her jaws around my arm. I screamed when her teeth sank deep. Tears sprang to my eyes from the pain. There was victory in the wolf's eyes. Prudence was going to tear my limb off.

My mind was filled with the image of a huge white wolf. The same wolf from my dreams. *Release me,* my inner animal begged.

My body grew hot. Sharp pain rushed through me.

Somewhere in the distance, I heard a scream, followed by another. Then I realized the shrieks were mine.

Hot, scorching pain whipped across my skin. My bones felt like they were breaking and rearranging. My muscles were stretching and rippling.

Prudence's wolf released her grip on my arm, backing away with her tail between her legs.

What the hell is happening?

I glanced around the mob. Everyone's eyes locked on me.

Quinn stepped forward and then stopped. He cocked his head to the side as he stared at me.

Why is he staring at me like I've grown two heads?

Something rammed into me like a freight train. It was Prudence.

I landed hard on the grass. Grunting, I pushed to my four furry feet.

Four?

Furry?

What the hell?

Prudence came at me again. I barely got out of the way.

As I turned to face my nemesis, Prudence rushed me again, this time sinking her teeth into my side.

I shook my body hard, forcing Prudence to let go, and then I attacked her hindquarters. Prudence's wolf whimpered, backing away.

I waited for her next move.

Prudence attacked once more.

I leaped up, catching Prudence's neck between my jaws. Clamping down hard, I tasted her acrid blood before shaking her wolf, slamming her to the ground.

Prudence wheezed, trying to lift her body, but failed. A pain-filled whine escaped her lips.

I hovered above her, snapping and growling.

Her eyes widened with fear and defeat.

I snapped my teeth again, ready for the kill.

Show no mercy. Kill her, my wolf demanded.

I growled down at Prudence. Wheezing, she rolled onto her back, presenting me with her neck and belly.

Kill. Her, my wolf ordered.

I froze. *Killing Prudence is not who I am.*

I am the alpha female.

I must show mercy to the weak.

Touching my nose to Prudence's belly, I stepped away. *Mercy.*

The crowd erupted with loud clapping, stomping, and chanting, repeating "Imani" over and over.

My gaze panned the area, taking in the ruckus. I snorted. Those fuckers deserved my middle finger. Exhausted, all I wanted to do was shift back into my human form and put this fucking duel shit behind me.

But I had no clue how to shift back to my human form.

What if I stay stuck like this forever?

Calm, I heard a male voice command in my head.

Quinn?

Yes. Change, Imani.

I shook my head. *I don't know how.*

I will guide you, he reassured me.

My panic faded.

He continued to speak into my mind, *Think of your human form, Imani.*

My human body came to the forefront of my mind.

That's it, Imani, Quinn soothed. *Now think of how you felt when you shifted into your beast.*

I can't, Quinn.

My body felt like I was swimming against the tide in a turbulent sea. I was tired and wanted to give up, letting the darkness take me, dragging me under.

Shift, Imani! he ordered.

Something snapped inside my head. I could feel him merging with my mind, calling to my beast, forcing her to change. A ripple of pain rushed through my limbs, then everything around me faded, and I was on my knees with Quinn hugging me.

"Imani?" he asked with eyes filled with worry.

"Did I really just hear your voice in my mind?" I whispered.

"Yes, we are one, and we can now mind-speak."

"Holy shit!" My eyes widened. "And I shifted."

"Into an Arctic wolf," he informed me with a twinkle in his eyes.

"Well, I guess that settles the question about what type of shifter I am."

Quinn placed a hard kiss on my lips. "Yes, it does, mate." When he pulled me to my feet, I realized I was completely naked before the entire Black Forest community.

"Well, this is embarrassing," I croaked, standing with my ass and breasts on full display.

"No." Quinn stroked my cheek. "This is spectacular and beautiful, just like you."

CHAPTER 31
IMANI

EIGHT MONTHS LATER… ON A FULL MOON

"You okay?" Quinn asked.

"Nope," I replied honestly. "There is nothing normal about a mating ceremony that requires us to get freaky naughty in the forest while the entire town waits for us to climax."

"I'll be quick." He squeezed my hand reassuringly as the floor-length gold cloaks we each wore swished around our ankles while we walked barefoot across the same spot where I'd had my duel against Prudence months ago.

I snorted. "You and I don't have quick sex."

He laughed. "I ain't going to apologize for loving everything about my mate, including her body."

I rolled my eyes skyward. "The things I do for you, Alpha."

He kissed my hand. "And I love you for it, my alpha female."

I squeezed his hand, loving his term of endearment. Our relationship had blossomed after I'd won the duel against Prudence. And my time in the Ridge had been a whirlwind of activities, including getting to know the pack, the town, helping Piper with the B and B, and last but not least, settling in with my fated mate, Quinn.

I was still getting acclimated to Others' traditions and laws, and most were plain crazy and antiquated, including this mating-ceremony requirement.

Although Quinn had claimed, mated, and marked me, that wasn't enough to satisfy busybody townsfolk. According to Others' tradition, because we were an alpha pair, Quinn and I had to be joined via a full-moon mating ceremony witnessed by the residents of Black Forest instead of having a private event.

A slight murmur went through the throng as Quinn led me to the center of the circle where Freya, wearing a skintight floor-length dress, waited. The entire town was here. I smiled when I saw my family—Piper, Freya, Nyx, the Bane pack, Izzy, and Rose —dressed to the nines as they gathered for our ceremony. I nearly burst out with laughter when I saw that Nyx, Rose, and Izzy were each wearing a white T-shirt with the slogan GLITTER IS ALWAYS AN OPTION paired with a glittery gold leather skirt.

Freya raised her arms skyward while looking up at the bright, full moon. "Luna. Goddess of the moon," she began loudly, her voice carrying across the clearing. "We are here tonight to ask for your blessing in joining our town alpha, Quinn, and his alpha female, Imani."

Lowering her arms, she eyed Quinn. "Quinn Bane, who is this female that you ask to mate?"

He squeezed my hand lightly and replied, "Imani Parker."

"Will anyone challenge Quinn Bane's right to mate this female?" Freya asked.

Tensing, he narrowed his eyes as he swept them over the gathered audience as if daring anyone to challenge him. No one did.

"Imani Parker, who is this male that you ask to mate?" Freya asked.

"Quinn Bane," I answered.

"Will anyone challenge Imani Parker's right to mate this male?"

I glanced around. No one spoke.

Freya nodded. "Quinn Bane, will you take this female you have claimed to be your fated mate forever?"

"Yes."

She asked the same question of me about Quinn. "Yes," I responded.

Freya raised her hands to the sky. Her fingers slowly glowed with a bright white light that replicated the color of the moon.

Freya nodded again. "By the light that shines from my fingers, Luna approves of this mating of our town alpha to this alpha female. Take your mate, Quinn Bane." She stepped forward, giving each of us a light kiss on the cheek before declaring, "Before the council, the town, and your pack, we declare you officially mated.

"This night is a new beginning for our town." Freya peered at the gathering of townsfolk. "May our unmated males find their fated mates. And may the coupling between our alphas be strong, happy, and loving."

Clapping and howls erupted into the night.

Piper had tears streaming down her cheeks when she grabbed me into a tight embrace. "I love you, Imani. Welcome to the family."

"And I love you," I returned, hugging her for dear life before stepping back.

Emmett, Brody, Mack, Rhett, and Jasper each took turns hugging me, then clapped Quinn on the back.

Nyx, Rose, and Izzy grinned, then screamed, "Congratulations!" in unison while throwing copious amounts of pink and green glitter on me.

"Ugh. Glitter." I swiped my arm playfully at them. They leaped out of reach with wide grins on their faces.

"What do we do now?" I asked Quinn.

"We go into the forest and complete our private joining." He grabbed my hand.

Hand in hand, we strode through the crowd and across the dewy grass. After a few minutes, we made it to the edge of the forest and then weaved our way inside, traipsing over the mossy green forest floor that felt like carpet against the bottoms of my bare feet.

"The forest is so beautiful at night," I mused aloud.

"That it is," Quinn agreed. "Just a few more minutes and we'll reach the spot for our joining."

My nose twitched at the smell of damp moss intermingled with the sweet scent of flowers. Moonlight filtered through the canopy, casting an otherworldly glow over the ground and large trees.

"We're close," he said.

I could hear the gurgling of water before we reached the small patch of earth, overgrown with deep green moss, alongside a large lake.

"Are you ready?" he asked.

"Yes."

Quinn reached for the clasp of my cloak, undoing it before pushing the material off my shoulders. I wiggled, allowing the garment to slide to the grass. I shivered as the chilled air touched my naked body, causing my nipples to pucker. Feeling completely exposed, I panned my eyes around for anyone lurking behind the trees.

"We are alone, Imani. Eyes on me."

I refocused on him, and he stroked my face with his hand, relaxing me.

I unclasped his cloak, pushing it off his shoulders. He shucked it and stood before me naked. Lust raced through me as I stared at my man's sculpted nakedness and enormous cock jutting away from his body.

"On the ground, Imani."

Doing as told, I lay on my back. He settled over me. I moaned as he molded my breasts with his hands while sucking and biting one rock-hard nipple until I was writhing and grinding beneath him. He journeyed down my body, pausing now and then to nip and suck at small sensitive sections of skin.

He took a minute to look at me lying there, trembling and wet, ready for him to take and possess. I gasped as he cocked my hips, kissing my hot folds. His thick tongue swirled around my secret center, repeatedly flicking it before sinking inside my throbbing core. My ass flew up, and he held me still, demolishing me unrelentingly with his wicked, clever tongue.

His soft rumbles vibrated against my clit, heightening the pleasure, almost sending me over the edge. His tongue continued to pillage my tight depths until I threaded my fingers through his hair and tugged hard. He snarled in the back of his throat.

"Please," I begged.

He froze, peering up at my face, before kneeling between my legs, gripping my hips, and positioning his erection at my warm folds. "Please what?"

"Please fuck me."

As if my plea splintered his self-control, he wrapped his fingers around his shaft, poised at my entrance. He was breathing hard as he looked into my eyes while gently pushing against me, giving me time to get used to his wide girth.

He leaned down and breathed against my lips, "You are mine." His nostrils flared as he inched his cock into me.

Wrapping my legs around his waist, I drove my hips up to meet him as he slammed into me. My muscles clamped around his massive fullness, and then he took me.

I let go and completely surrendered to Quinn.

This man was mine, and I was totally his.

Pressing his forehead against mine, he moved hard and fast. Squeezing my thighs tight around his hips, I clung to him for dear life, riding the wave of lust coiling through me. He brought his hands up to my breasts, gently cupping them, sliding his thumbs over the aching brown peaks. I gripped his ass, my nails digging deep.

"All of you. Mine," I growled, wrapping my legs around him. "I want to ride you."

He rolled over, still inside me. He was sitting up with us face-to-face while I straddled him. Leaning forward, I placed my arms around his neck, swiveling my hips with shallow, fast thrusts, allowing myself to sink onto Quinn every fifth thrust.

Quinn groaned at the deep penetration, his callused hands on my hips. On the edge of an orgasm, I nibbled my way down his throat. My gums throbbed and incisors lengthened. Settling in the juncture of his neck and shoulder, I scraped my teeth over the spot before biting down, breaking the skin. Quinn roared. I climaxed hard. Licking over the area, I leaned back to eye him.

"Mine," I growled.

Quinn's eyes were amber when he ordered, "On your hands and knees, Imani."

I obeyed, sliding off him and getting down on all fours.

Quinn crouched down behind me, nudging my knees apart. I trembled when his fingers danced along my spine, then over my ass.

"Do you take me as your mate, Imani?"

"Yes, I do."

I moaned when his cock brushed the wet and ready opening of my pussy.

"I take you as my mate, Imani Parker. I take you as my other half, the mother of my children, the only female in my bed," he said clearly.

Now it was my turn to say the same to Quinn.

"I take you as my mate, Quinn Bane. I take you as my other half, the father of my children, the only male in my bed."

Quinn pushed his thick length into my body.

I dug my fingernails into the moss beneath us.

Quinn sank his incisors into my shoulder as his cock moved hard and fast inside my hot slit.

An achy heat engulfed me as he pumped steadily.

"Quinn!" I cried out as my orgasm washed over me. Quinn bit down harder. His thrusts grew faster, and then he growled. His cock grew larger inside me. He stilled, allowing me to adjust to the enormous width.

Relax, he said into my mind.

My muscles loosened, and he began thrusting again. I shuddered, coming apart under his sensual fucking. My stomach tightened as my orgasm tore through me. Quinn grunted as his seed shot into me over and over again.

He released his grip on my shoulder, licking at my bite mark before slowly lowering us to the ground and rolling us over onto our sides. Pressing my back against his chest, I relaxed into his embrace while he was still hard and buried deep inside me.

"So we're officially mated?" I whispered.

"Yes, my beautiful mate." Quinn gently pulled out of me, before standing and extending a hand to help me up.

"Now we shift," Quinn said.

We both called to our inner beasts and shifted into our wolf form.

Side by side, we stood. One large black wolf and a smaller white wolf.

What do we do now? I asked, speaking into his mind.

Run with me, Imani.

CHAPTER 32
QUINN

We tore off across the grass, deeper into the forest.

Follow me, I directed.

It didn't take us long to make it to one of the many natural hot springs in the forest. Imani shifted back into her human form before plunging into the warm, soothing water. "Freaking glitter," she mumbled and washed off.

I shifted into my human form before walking up behind her. Sniffing at her neck, I noticed that her scent was changing. She would go into heat again soon.

"What's with the sniffing?" Imani swatted at me playfully. "Stop it."

I turned her to face me. "I love you." She was my world and my heart.

"And I love you," she whispered, staring up at me.

She was silent for a moment, and I watched her as the moonlight shone across her dark skin.

"Imani? What are you thinking about?"

"I'm so happy, Quinn, and I have so much. A man who respects and loves me, a real family. But I'm just so terrified that it could be snatched away."

"Never." I kissed her quick and hard. "You're stuck with us forever." Grabbing her face, I said, "So you'll have to marry me."

She stared at me with lips pursed in disbelief.

I continued, "It can be a small ceremony, with just the pack and Freya, Nyx, Rose, and Izzy."

"Quinn, Others don't believe in marriage."

"But I do. And you do too." I ran my fingers through her hair. "Imani, you've done so much to adapt to this fucked-up town and residents. Let's do something for you, for us." I paused. "Imani Parker, will you marry me?"

She smiled up at me, locking her arms around my neck. "Yes, Quinn Bane. I'll marry you."

She wrapped her legs around my waist when I lifted her up. "She said yes!" I yelled into the night while spinning around.

She laughed. "Quit it. You're making me dizzy."

I stopped, kissing her hard. "Imani, you don't know how happy you make me. Every morning that I wake up with you in my arms and every night that I go to sleep with you by my side fill me with so much love and happiness."

Tears formed at the corners of her eyes.

"Why are you crying?" I asked.

"They're tears of love and joy, because the only place that I want to be for the rest of my life is with you."

"Forever," I whispered, staring at the only woman to complete me.

"Yes. Forever, Alpha."

EPILOGUE

RHETT

"Sheriff Ward, can't you do something about Sam?" Dean, a skunk-shifter, demanded as he sat in the chair across my desk from me. "Ever since I kicked Sam out of the Sleepy Skunk Motel, he keeps showing up at my place at random times of the week, making threats against me and my mate, Agnes."

I rubbed the bridge of my nose, trying to ignore the loud snoring sounds in my head coming from my inner jaguar.

"Dean, we've staked out your place several times, but he's not going to show up if he smells us there. He's not that stupid. He's an elusive motherfucker who can't be found until he pops his head out of whatever hidey-hole he's taking refuge in now."

Sam was always causing trouble. His last attempt had been last year when he'd riled up the townsfolk after Imani, our town and pack alpha female, arrived inside the Ridge.

"Well, something's got to give," Dean complained. "Last time he showed up, he threatened to kill my mate if I didn't give him a room." He rubbed his eyes. "I think something's wrong with him. He's acting pretty crazy."

I scoffed. "Sam was born crazy."

Dean shook his head. "No. This is different. I've seen this

kind of thing before. You know, when a shifter has the feral sickness."

I leaned forward in my chair, eyeing Dean. "Feral sickness?"

It wasn't unusual for unmated male shifters to turn violent and lose touch with their human side, slowly going feral because they couldn't find their fated mate.

"Yes, Protector. I've seen the signs—glossy, wild eyes, talking gibberish—of going feral in some of my kin." Dean gave me a bleak look. "Before they ran deep into the forest, never to be seen again."

Dean's new perspective on the Sam situation gave me food for thought. *Is Sam's erratic behavior escalating because he's going feral?*

"Sam will show up in Main Square sooner than later," I promised. My extensive military training taught me that patience was a virtue. "He loves attention and stirring the pot."

And when he shows his ass in town, I'm going to lock him up and throw away the key.

"I know that you're stretched thin with just you and Mack, but can you continue checking on my place?" His mouth worked. "I'm terrified that Sam's going to do something to hurt Agnes and me."

"When I took this job as the Protector of the Ridge, I swore to serve and protect all the residents of this town, regardless of who they are and what they've done. And I'm going to continue doing just that."

"Thanks, Protector. I'll let Agnes know not to worry."

I rose to my feet, and so did Dean.

"Good. You do that," I finished as we shook hands.

Dean turned, shuffling out of my office.

Plopping down in my chair, I propped my booted legs on the edge of my desk, running a hand through my hair.

Even over six years after relocating here, I still felt like an outsider, and getting the residents to trust and confide in me was a work in progress. But I loved my job as the sheriff—aka Protector—even if it was a major change in lifestyle after spending years traveling all over the world while serving in an elite military unit with my band of brothers—Quinn, Mack, Emmett, Jasper, and Brody.

Taking a swig of my now-cold coffee, I nearly choked when my beast snored even louder in my head.

Get the hell up, I verbally nudged him. *We're on duty.*

I'm bored, he complained. *Nothing ever happens here.*

As it should be, I snapped.

Except for the clusterfuck Sam had started when Imani had arrived, things in the Black Forest had been calm and quiet, and that was how I liked it.

Wake me up when it's time for dinner, my inner animal demanded, then went silent.

I sighed heavily. The relationship between my inner beast and me was tense. He was pissed off because—his words, not mine—*You're a lazy ass for giving up the search for our fated mate.*

His accusation couldn't be further from the truth.

Laziness wasn't my problem. It was fear.

I'd already failed as the protector of my baby sister, Maggie; there was no way I wanted to add a fated mate to my list of failures.

Shifters of Black Forest Ridge isn't over yet, not by a long shot. Get ready for Book #2, Rhett's story by grabbing SHIFTERS OF BLACK FOREST RIDGE: RHETT right now.

WANT A LITTLE MORE OF QUINN'S STORY?

Get deleted scenes from Shifters of Black Forest Ridge: Quinn, right now by joining Sedona's mailing list.

ABOUT THE AUTHOR

USA TODAY BESTSELLING AUTHOR SEDONA VENEZ lives in New York City with her former military hubby—hooah—and their fur babies. She loves writing sizzling, sexy intricate stories about strong but broken characters who push limits, overcome their fears and risk it all for love.

Sedona loves to connect with readers!
www.sedonavenez.com